LIFTING WEIGHTS

LIFTING WEIGHTS

Judy McCrosky

thistledown press

Thistledown Press Ltd.
410 2nd Avenue North
Saskatoon, Saskatchewan, S7K 2C3
www.thistledownpress.com

Library and Archives Canada Cataloguing in Publication

McCrosky, Judy, 1956–, author
Lifting weights / Judy McCrosky.

Short stories.
Issued in print and electronic formats.
ISBN 978-1-77187-105-1 (paperback). – ISBN 978-1-77187-106-8 (html).– ISBN 978-1-77187-107-5 (pdf)

I. Title.

PS8575.C736L54 2016 C813'.54 C2016-905244-3
C2016-905245-1

Cover and book design by Jackie Forrie
Printed and bound in Canada

Canada Council for the Arts Conseil des Arts du Canada

Canada

Thistledown Press gratefully acknowledges the financial assistance of the Canada Council for the Arts, the Saskatchewan Arts Board, and the Government of Canada for its publishing program.

Warm thanks to the members of Critical Mass in Saskatoon and of Clarion West 96, for your support and critiques over the years. I couldn't do it without you.

And special thanks to Thistledown Press, for believing in me when you published my first book, and for believing in me still.

CONTENTS

Horsepower

ARABELLA WATCHED AS THE two Securipooches delicately sniffed beneath each other's metal tail. Behind them stood three identical workbenches with matte grey surfaces and shiny grey sinks.

Everything is always the same, Arabella thought. The ad men all in black and the scientists all in white. Outside, the same flat prairie landscape and me in here, as I always am, looking for a story.

"They're a resounding success." Emmanuel, CEO of the Trumpeter Swan ad agency, smoothed his droopy mustache and then rested his hands on the platform conveniently presented by his bulging stomach.

"Securipooches provide safety to homewners the world over." He stood in the centre of the biochem lab like a king surveying his realm.

Arabella tapped her pen on her screen, imagining headlines: *Home Security Going To The Dogs? Dog Genes Outsmart Criminal Genes.* But the most important words would come after the headline: *By Arabella Esther.*

Her boss thought he could run the science beat by waiting for scientists to call him. He never went out after a story. Well, if this product were as big as its mouthpieces implied, the story just might inspire Glen Townsend, the paper's editor, to name a new senior science reporter.

She glanced at Clive, the photographer, as his face twisted in an embarrassed grimace. One of the Securipooches had buried its nose in his crotch. She hid a smile behind her hand.

Emmanuel pulled the creature away and shooed it towards the workbenches. Clive aimed his holocam at it to hide his blush.

"So sorry," Emmanuel said jovially. "Sometimes genes code for more than one trait. It appears that this sniffing," he wrinkled his nose, "is connected to territory defense or loyalty to owners."

"Love and protection," Arabella said to her screen. Everything she'd learned showed that people grew to love the dogs with metal bodies and beating hearts. But the real story was the biogrid, and it hadn't been easy finding even the little information she had. Last year's Nobel Prize in Artificial Intelligence had been expected to go to the biogrid's inventor, Dr. Javed Syed. Instead, a woman who'd created an intelligent hairdryer received the prize. Arabella heard later that Dr. Syed had withdrawn his invention from public distribution, saying it needed more work. "Tell me about the biogrid," she said, pointing to the Securipooches who were now trying to dig through the floor.

"The biogrid," Emmanuel said, "will do more to change the way humans interact with their world than has any other invention."

"The biogrid," said Arabella, hoping he'd get on with it, "has enabled genetic components to interact with machines."

"Exactly." He nodded. "For years we've added machine parts to living beings. Now we can add human, animal, or even plant traits to machines."

Plant genes? Maybe she could get a mechanical implant in her skull and use plant genes to replace her dark wiry hair with a golden flow of corn silk. "Have human genes been used — ?" Arabella asked.

Emmanuel continued as if he hadn't heard her. "Securipooches are an engineering marvel, but they're only — "

"Have human genes been used in this way?"

Emmanuel sighed. "Would you build a ship to carry you to the stars before anyone had yet walked on the moon?"

"I would," she stuck out her chin, "if I thought I could. Nothing's accomplished until someone tries."

He was all smiles again. "And just look what we've accomplished by trying. The Securipooch encompasses the strengths of both dog and machine. They're faster and stronger than dogs, they can bite through a two-inch steel bar, and yet they play with little children and lick their owners' hands."

"What kind of saliva do they have? Motor oil?"

Emmanuel opened his mouth to reply, but she held up a hand. "Never mind. Bad joke. Weren't mice the donors of the first mammal genes used with the biogrid?"

Emmanuel rubbed one shoe on the material of his gaitered trousers.

"The biogrid," Arabella told Clive, "was placed in a computer mouse."

"You said it yourself," Emmanuel said. "Nothing's accomplished until something is tried. The biogrid enables genes to become part of the machine, to produce muscles and other proteins, and use the machine's metal frame as skeletal support. There's even a brain of a sort created, or a neurocommand centre, as we prefer to call it. Our bio-machines are a most impressive accomplishment."

Arabella grinned. "The computer mouse was a joke. It had a tendency to hide in shadowy corners, scuttle around the edges of the room, and it also, as I recall, squeaked quite becomingly."

Clive laughed. "Good thing it didn't have teeth."

Emmanuel glared at them both. "Just how, may I ask, did you learn about that?"

"I'm good at research," Arabella said.

"Well," Emmanuel smoothed his belted jacket. "All your research hasn't netted you the real story."

"And what might that be?"

"Horsepower."

Clive was filming the Securipooches, one of whom turned around three times and lay down. Arabella shoved her notescreen into her bag. "Horsepower has been around forever."

"Not like this, it hasn't." Emmanuel seemed unfazed by her preparations to leave. "Imagine this: a car that will fill your mind with images of muscle and grace, of wind streaming through a silken mane. A car with a personality, a car you will love, and that will love you back."

Arabella paused in the act of inflating her coat's insulation layer.

"Cars have been around a long time." Emmanuel's voice was as silken as any mane. "They're so familiar we don't think about them. They're just there. We get in, tell it where we want to go, and turn on the morning paper. But there was a time when people loved to drive. That time is with us once again."

"Okay." Arabella shrugged, but her heart began to pound. Maybe this was the story that would get her noticed. "Good hook. You've got me listening."

"Driving is no fun because we aren't involved with our vehicle."

"It's safer, now. With road sensors for guidance and to control speed, traffic accidents are down to almost zero."

"But," Emmanuel lifted a finger and waved it under her nose, "is safety all people want from life? I don't think so. Near the end of the 20th century, the speed limit in the USA was lowered to 55 mph. Fatalities decreased, but a few years later those speed limits were back up. Why?"

"I'm sure you're going to tell me."

"Because people wanted to drive, that's why. They wanted power and speed. They wanted to feel the car, be part of something greater than they could be alone. Driving now is like sitting at home on a sofa. Horsepower will change that, will return us to the days when driving was fun. And just think what an increase in car sales will do for our economy."

"Are you telling me," Arabella asked slowly, "that someone has used horse genes on a biogrid, and put it into a car?"

Emmanuel stroked his mustache and smiled.

ഇഇഇ

Kitsy lovingly ran her hand down the hood of her pale cream car. Its front end was longer and narrower than those of modern cars and the back end was rounded, the fenders giving the impression of bunched muscles ready to spring. Solar strips ringed the roof, but there was also an intake valve for hydrogen fuel centred at the back. The car nickered and butted Kitsy, gently, with its bumper.

Its body shone in the sunlight, but not with the hard gleam of metal. A fine coat of hairs contributed to the colour. The front headlights, Arabella knew, concealed cameras so the car could see.

"Can you tell me," she asked, notescreen held ready, "about your relationship with your car?"

The car's side mirrors flicked forward, as if listening to this unfamiliar voice.

"Get in," Kitsy said. "I'll show you."

Eyeing the side mirrors nervously, Arabella slid into the passenger seat. The upholstery was also pale cream, but unlike the exterior skin, the seat appeared to be made of a durable fabric, not of anything that could move on its own.

"I love my car." Kitsy leaned forward for the retinal scan that started the engine. "I've named her Shining Sands Rani Princess in honour of her Arabian roots."

"Isn't Rani an Indian term?" Arabella asked, but the car started moving and Kitsy didn't seem to have heard.

The car sounded like every other car, a muted machine purr, as it merged with the suburban traffic. "Are horses and cars a good mix?"

"The best," Kitsy gushed. Arabella knew the woman was twenty-eight, but her high-pitched voice and giggles made her seem much younger. "Only three of us got Arabians."

Arabella searched her mind for a question that would elicit a useful, or even intelligent, answer. She knew each Horsepower had been created with genes from its own individual horse, but discussing the pros and cons of various horse breeds didn't seem like it would lead to headline-quality quotes. "How were you chosen to be an owner in this pilot project?"

"I guess it's because I just love horses so much." Kitsy clasped her hands together in ecstasy. "I can't think why else. Can you?" Her blue eyes were wide.

Arabella masterfully ignored this opening as Kitsy prattled on about written tests. "Only multiple choice. Isn't that lucky?" She went on to describe games she had to play with the testers. "One was where we had to pretend we were driving back in the days before guidance and sensors. They thought I'd be scared, but I wasn't. I loved it. And I only hit two traffic cones!"

"All the owners were tested?" Arabella asked. The car was leaving Kitsy's neighborhood, an area of two-storey houses that all looked alike, although they were different colours.

"Yes." Kitsy stroked the dashboard above the GPS display. "This is her favourite place to be scratched."

"Have you met the others?"

"Not yet. I look forward to seeing what colour they all are."

"The owners?"

Kitsy, busily at work with her nails, each carefully filed into minute serrations, looked over, her thin face puzzled. The car slowed for an intersection. Kitsy's face cleared, and she laughed. "No, I meant the other Horsepowers. Emmanuel and

Dr. Syed felt it would be best if each owner and Horsepower developed a personal bond before we get together as a group."

"Dr. Syed?" The biogrid inventor refused all requests for interviews.

"He sent a message." Kitsy's eyes, heavily shadowed with orange, turned dreamy. Little gold horseshoes flashed on and off within the makeup. "He told us our vehicles were a new breed, and that they'd teach us about being alive. And I do feel more alive now. I do. I knew we were soulmates the moment we met." The car moved into an intersection, stopping at the embedded turn line until the road system gave it permission to turn left.

"You've met Dr. Syed?"

"No, silly," Kitsy giggled. "When Shining Sands Rani Princess and I first met."

Arabella gritted her teeth. "In your experience, how do the horse traits affect your car's performance?" The car turned and moved into the guidance system's usual ten feet behind the car ahead.

"The horse and machine traits mesh perfectly." Despite Kitsy's earnest voice, Arabella was sure she was repeating something Emmanuel had said. "After all," Kitsy continued, "horses have worked with people for thousands of years, providing transportation, muscle, and companionship. There is no other animal so well suited for — "

Something huge and noisy crashed beside them. A construction crane had dropped a crate filled with steel beams. That's all Arabella had time to see as the world tipped and she fell heavily against the seat back.

As her feet flipped up above her head, she thought fleetingly that perhaps seat belts should still be mandatory. Then the world became level again, the switch just as sudden, and Arabella found herself in a heap on her seat, one leg twisted painfully under her hips, only to be hurled against the seat back as the car accelerated fast. The guidance system quickly caught it and the vehicle slowed to the speed of the others around it.

Arabella gasped for air. Kitsy pouted. "That nasty construction site," she said. "It scared my poor Shining Sands Rani Princess."

Arabella blinked. "Scared? You mean . . . the car reared up?"

"Of course. And then she ran. It's what horses do when they're scared. But the mean old guidance system didn't let you run." She stroked the dashboard. "There there, sweetie, it's okay. I won't let anything hurt you."

This is nuts, Arabella thought. But the car gave a soft rumble and the dashboard molded itself to better fit Kitsy's caress, and Arabella wondered.

ꟻꟻꟻ

She interviewed three other Horsepower owners. The cars all behaved just like cars, and the owners spoke passionately about the need to disable the guidance systems and sensors. One owner, a retired policeman who wore a cowboy hat and a big-buckled belt, said, "They need to be free. It's a crime, keeping these cars penned up like this. They've got to be true to their nature."

But they aren't natural, Arabella thought, as she travelled in her own car to the newsroom. All around her cars moved at the same speed, equidistant from each other.

The newsroom was chaos, as usual. People sat in tiny cubicles, or crammed together at desks. They talked into phones, into screens, to people on vids, even to people physically near them. Chairs rolled, squeaking and scraping, pens tapped screens, footsteps rapped the old lino floor.

Arabella wove her way through the maze of equipment and people. Her boss had asked to see her. What could Maximum Maximilian want? Did Max Max, so known because he always made sure he got maximum credit for any story, even if it was researched and written by someone else, have his eye on the biogrid? Her byline had appeared on each of her stories so far. That didn't mean, though, that Max hadn't been talking up his contribution, even though it was nil, to Glen.

"Arabella." He greeted her jovially, his small eyes gleaming, and her unease grew. He was actually a rather minimal person, thin and gangly, hair sparse although she could see from the reddish tufts that sprouted all over his head that he was trying yet another of the frequently advertised baldness cures. She supposed this was an improvement, as the last attempt had turned the little hair he had a lurid green.

"I wanted to congratulate you," he said, waving her into the only other seat in his small office. "You're doing good work."

Arabella forced her lips into a smile, and tried to relax her shoulders.

"I've been talking to our esteemed editor about you, in fact." He leaned forward, his hands rubbing together. "Told him how well you're coming along under my supervision.

Glen's very proud of you, said you've done a superb job with the biogrid. But now that it's drawing international attention . . . "

Arabella fought the urge to close her eyes in preparation for the blow. "Yes?"

Max beamed, his thin lips revealing perfectly capped teeth. "Trumpeter Swan called today. Emmanuel insisted on speaking to the Senior Science writer. He told me that since the pilot project with the Horsepowers has gone so well, he's ready to introduce the cars to the world. There's going to be a rally, with all twenty Horsepowers showing their stuff. Isn't that exciting?"

Emannuel, Arabella thought. I dug him up as a contact. Disloyal bastard.

Max put a serious expression on and leaned forward in a fatherly way. "I want you to attend the event. You seem to like participating in the outside world." He shuddered. "But I'll write it up. Glen felt it was too important to trust to anyone other than me. Keep in mind every paper in the world will be covering this event. See if you can dig up something new. You'll get research credit, of course."

"Something new?" Arabella said through clenched teeth. "For a research credit?"

Max nodded. "Go for it. Something like an interview with the biogrid's inventor." He laughed. "Hell, pull that off and I'll share the byline with you. That guy's been as slippery as — "

Arabella shot to her feet. "So I'll do all the work, and you'll reap the glory."

"Since I know you love to be busy," Max Max continued quickly, "I've got a new assignment for you. Multisound Labs called, they've got a new vinyl record under production. It's an important story, I'm counting on you."

"This is so like you." Arabella kept talking. "Well, it's not going to happen. Not this time. Not again."

"I don't know what you're on about." He pouted. "It's not like you to be so feisty, Arabella."

"It's exactly like me." She kept her tone even only with a great effort. "My feistiness is the reason I find so many stories. Stories that you steal, because you're too busy sucking up to Glen to do your job."

"I'd be careful if I were you," he said, stroking his chin. "We have to follow protocol. I am senior to you. Glen knows best." He pointed to the door of his office, and Arabella spun around. Standing there, sporting a flinty little smile, was Glen Townsend.

"I don't like being careful." She stared into Max's eyes and then Glen's. Normally the editor's flinty grey eyes and high-cheekboned face made her stammer and stutter, not knowing what to say. Not this time. "You never find stories, Max, because your whole life is spent in your home, your car, or here in your office. What are you so afraid of? Good journalism doesn't come from being careful. A new angle won't appear while you're one of the crowd. You have to get out there and take risks." And if this is the sort of newspaper where careful people are encouraged, then I don't want to be part of it. She heard the words in her head, felt them pushing to come out, but she pressed her lips together, and left.

People clustered around the edge of the newsroom that held the department offices, all trying to look busy, listening for all they were worth. As she pushed her way through them, she realized her anger was now directed at herself.

ඞඞඞ

A wide street downtown had been closed to all traffic but Horsepowers. A boulevard with trees and tubs of flowers slit the road down the middle, and tall faceless buildings lined either side. The Horsepowers were parked along the street, each with its owner sitting inside, door open so as to be better able to show off the vehicle and answer questions from the admiring people clustered thickly around.

Clive headed into one of the buildings for overhead shots, leaving Arabella to circulate.

Some sort of signal must have passed between the twenty owners, because they began driving down one side of the boulevard and up the other, a triumphant circle of cars.

They didn't look like normal traffic. The distances between them weren't equal, and the cars changed speed. A roan pulled up behind a grey and passed. Arabella blinked. Could the owners have disabled the guidance system and distance sensors in their vehicles?

A sorrel car moved behind a white one until its bumper was scant inches from the car in front. The white turned and the two faced each other, side mirrors pinned back.

The standoff blocked the road, and the other Horsepowers grouped behind. Clive reappeared beside Arabella as Emmanuel, wearing a top hat, ran across the boulevard, ducking so branches wouldn't knock his hat off. "What have you done?" he cried. "How is this possible?"

Arabella wondered the same thing. No one had ever been able to disable safety features. Encryption, locks, and multiple redundancy made sure of that.

A slight man with coffee-coloured skin stood not far from Arabella, his dark eyes intent on the cars. A small smile appeared beneath his plaited mustache.

Arabella nudged Clive, excitement tightening her chest. "That's Dr. Syed." Clive lifted his holocam.

Emmanuel had reached the cars and was waving his arms and yelling. An owner, a small elderly man, got out and began yelling back. He was joined by other owners, including Kitsy dressed all in yellow satin, the latest rebel clothes.

"Yes," the old man cried, and his voice rang triumphantly. "We have disabled all that kept our Horsepowers enslaved."

"Other cars may be happy with a life of safe speeds and obedience to rules," someone else yelled. It was the cowboy she'd interviewed. "Our Horsepowers will never submit."

"Cars aren't capable of happiness or unhappiness," Emmanuel shouted, but he was drowned out by the owners, all of whom had left their vehicles. Kitsy jumped onto the hood of a chestnut car, but was quickly pulled down by the elderly owner, who seemed concerned that her clogs would hurt the vehicle.

Emmanuel, joined by other ad men, yelled. The owners yelled. The smile on Dr. Syed's face grew. The two cars with pinned-back mirrors put their back ends toward each other, and one suddenly kicked with its back tires. The other cars moved about, some snapping with their hoods, others using their radiator fans to blow into each other's grilles.

Arabella was glad she'd come. This was fun. But now it was time to get Dr. Syed to talk to her. "Horses," she said loudly to Clive, "get to know each other by blowing into one another's nostrils."

Dr. Syed glanced over. "You know horses?" His accent rounded vowels and turned his words into music.

Arabella shook her head ruefully. "Based on what I've seen of the Horsepowers, I wish I did."

He nodded in understanding. Arabella fumbled in her bag for her notescreen. No way she'd share a byline for this interview.

But Dr. Syed was turning his attention back to the cars. Arabella, desperate to keep him talking, said the first words she could think of. "Do you like horses?"

"I admire horses," he said, "as I do all living things."

"You mean animals?"

"Living means being true to one's nature. Thinking, but not as we now define it. A tree doesn't accept what other trees tell it to think. A worm has worm thoughts, and no amount of people trying to tell it otherwise will prevent it from burrowing into dirt. A horse," he gestured to the Horsepowers, "has horse thoughts. Trees, worms, and horses are alive."

"You create machines that think?"

He swept an arm out, taking in the identical facades on the buildings, the perfectly timed stream of traffic that could be seen in the distance. "That depends on how you define thinking." His brows came together. "They wanted to use my biogrid to make even more beings who think as they are instructed."

"You mean," Arabella said slowly, "you create beings that think for themselves? And that makes them alive?"

He looked away, his eyes now distant. "Do you have the freedom to be who you are?"

"How can I?" she asked, but he was once again intent on his creations. Arabella, following his gaze, saw the owners pushing the ad people away from the cars, Kitsy in front, pounding on Emmanuel's chest. His top hat was gone.

Despite the barrage, Emmanuel stood his ground. "We can't have a car that isn't obeying the rules of the road. Think of the increase in accidents. You don't want your nice new car hurt, do you?"

Arabella couldn't make out individual words amid the swell of anger from the owners. A thought struck her. "Are Horsepower owners alive?" she asked Dr. Syed. He said nothing, only smoothed his mustache and smiled, and she knew who'd disabled the safety features.

The cars had become a tight group, and they moved within the cluster uneasily, side mirrors flicking. A few of them lifted and stamped their tires.

A siren blared from the end of the block. "I've called the police," Emmanuel shouted. "What you've done to these vehicles is illegal and now you'll be arrested." The police cars, sirens in full wail, pulled up beside him, and one officer jumped out and shot a stun soundwave over the crowd.

The Horsepowers panicked. The increasing tension in the air, the sirens, and now this sudden loud noise sent them into chaos. Some reared, some bumped others, but they all ran, at first in many directions, some crashing through the trees on the boulevard, or knocking over the tubs of flowers.

Soon, though, as if they felt greater safety in numbers, they regrouped and raced together down the road, past people hurling themselves out of the way, until they vanished into the haze of traffic at the end of the blocked-off street.

The owners stood in a forlorn clump. "Come back," the cowboy yelled. "We wanted you free, but not like this."

Dr. Syed still stood beside Arabella. He spoke now, maybe to himself, maybe to the owners, Arabella couldn't tell. "Free?" he asked. "Free to follow your commands?" With that, he vanished into the crowd.

ᢒᢒᢒ

Arabella sat at her desk in the newsroom, watching the latest edition of the paper. "No trace has been found of any of the runaway vehicles," the screen told her. A holo of a brown Horsepower floated beside the projected words. 'Amazingly, they avoided accidents and made their way through traffic to the edge of the city,' said Emmanuel, responsible for promoting the new form of transportation. 'This is a very new technology. We still have high hopes for a car with which an owner can have a fulfilling relationship. Dr. Syed will no doubt have learned much from this experience, and he'll perfect his design very soon'." There was no other mention of Syed in the article.

"You did the right thing," a voice beside Arabella said. Clive stood by her elbow.

She sighed. "I guess so."

"He doesn't want people to know this design turned out exactly as he'd planned. He added a little chaos to a world that's too predictable. And he wouldn't have spoken to you if he'd known you were a journalist."

Arabella looked back at the screen, at the byline above the article, that read, *By Maximilian Thurston*. "Most of my successes as a journalist have come from listening to people who don't want to talk to me."

"But they do want to talk." He smiled at her, his brown eyes warm. "It's one of your gifts, Arabella, letting them know you want to listen." He turned to leave.

"Do we," she asked, grabbing his arm, "only think what we're told to think?"

He squeezed her shoulder. "Let me know when you want me to take pictures again."

She stared back at the screen. The holo now showed the cars racing away en masse. Across the room, Max Max sat in his windowed office, accepting congratulations on his dynamite story.

Arabella wished she had told Glen what he could do with her job. Was security really more important than being true to oneself? For many people it was, but the thought brought a wetness to her eyes, which she impatiently brushed away. "I am feisty," she said, thrusting out her chin. "Does that mean I'm a little bit alive?" As she switched off her computer, it comforted her to know that somewhere a herd of cars raced free across the prairie, the wind streaming cool and fresh over their windshields.

Shelter

You know how people often say of someone else that "he's not himself"? I say that about Ben, my son, and it's true.

He came home from the hospital one month ago today. During the weeks he was there I did what I had to. I sold myself. Not in the way you're thinking, not my body, although in a sense my house was my body, the outer structure I lived in. I sold my house and moved into this apartment. I had to, to pay the medical bills.

While he was in the hospital, he looked like himself. His face was the same — vivid blue eyes, freckles making tracks across his cheeks, the full lips that used to scowl at me. The injury hadn't affected the front of his skull. It was only at the back, the shaved hair, the tubes, the thick bandage that proved something had happened. That, and the vagueness in his eyes. He'd always been passionate, even in the days before he felt only anger. He was filled with life, and his eyes shone so fiercely that sometimes I needed to take a step back from their intensity.

Michael was flying in and I needed groceries. Before I left, I checked on Ben. He was asleep when I looked in his room.

At fourteen he was more than old enough to leave alone, aside from the fact that by the age of eleven, after Michael left, he'd lived his own life anyway, one which consisted of being home as little as possible, stealing cars, smoking anything flammable that could be rolled inside a cigarette paper . . .

I sighed as I started the Toyota. There was no sense in being nostalgic. And did I really want that Ben back? The one who screamed at me when I reminded him his curfew was midnight, but that was better than the days on end that he wouldn't speak to me at all? Yes. At least he would be Ben.

The car took me to the house, instead of to the grocery store. My house stood well back from the sidewalk, behind the hedge my mother planted. It made me angry, it looked so much like it always had — pale cream walls, brown shutters on the windows, steeply-pitched roof, flower boxes dripping red and yellow in front of the living-room windows. Colour that I'd put there, earlier this summer, when I'd planted petunias.

I'd painted the front door a pale blue. It would have been so natural to leave the car, walk up the path to that door, and insert my key to let myself in. Except that I'd given my house keys to the real estate agent, and probably the new owners had changed the lock. I could still picture myself going inside, hanging my jacket in the closet to the left of the small entrance hall, calling to see if Ben was home, even though he usually wasn't.

My house belonged here, on this street, but I no longer did. It looked so strong and solid that I felt insubstantial. The house was real and so I must be a ghost.

My ghost self floated into my house through the front door. No, it was more as if the house reached out and engulfed me, like a white blood cell envelops a bacterium. I'm in the front hall, then floating up the stairs. There's a long crack running up along the wall by the stairs.

I waft into my bedroom. The furniture is the same, as I'd sold the pieces too big for the apartment along with the house. The cherrywood four-poster bed is as beautiful as always, but the comforter is pink and flowery. It's nothing like the green and gold patchwork quilt my mother made me when I got married.

Then I see her. A small woman, with short curly blonde hair. She's standing between me and the window, her head thrown back, her fist curled at her mouth. Tears shine on her cheeks, and then she drops her head, her shoulders slump forward, and her body folds in around her grief.

I'm glad. I don't want her to be happy here.

I rise up through the roof and hang for moment, suspended over the home where I was born, where my mother was born, the only sheltering walls I've ever known. The apartment isn't a shelter, or rather, that's all it is, something to keep me warm and dry. Nothing more.

The cedar shakes have only been on for twenty-four years, but I see that many of them are cracked and warped. Maybe my house is struggling against the strangeness it now holds. Poor house.

I don't want it to suffer. I don't want it to lose shakes. But for a moment, my throat tightens as it fills with hate, and I hope my house hates the new woman as much as I do.

I'd refused to pick Michael up at the airport, but was home in time to open the door to him when he arrived in a taxi.

"Where is he?" Michael demanded. No "hello," or "how are you?" Why would I expect anything different?

"In his room," I said, adding, "he's looking forward to seeing you."

Of everything that had happened in the last few months, Ben saying that was the one thing that made me cry. I hadn't cried at all since the first horrible moment when the policeman told me that my son had been shot.

"Of course he's looking forward to seeing me." Michael dropped his suitcase and looked around, impatient that he didn't automatically know where to find his son.

Michael had often made me feel I slowed down the furious pace of his life. He always got what he wanted, and at first I was happy to be one of the things he swept up in his path. Now, though, a flame flared inside my stomach.

"Why of course?" I asked. "You have no idea how it hurt him when you left."

He cocked his head and stared at me as if I was a new form of pond scum on one of his slides.

"It's not," I went on, the words tripping over each other, "as if you've spent enough time with him during the last three years to know anything about him. You think Christmas cards and the occasional phone call are enough to maintain a relationship?"

He raised and lowered his shoulders in a sigh. "Are you going to start all this again?"

He hates you, I wanted to shout. He's hurt, but he never allowed his pains to show, not even as a little boy. So he's angry instead, and he hates you.

"I don't know if you understood," I said instead, "what I told you on the phone. Ben is . . . different." Michael hadn't been to see Ben while he was in the hospital. Michael had moved to the coast, a long way away, and his research samples had been at a critical stage. "Besides," he'd said to me, "it's not as if I can do anything that isn't already being done for him."

"You could be there for him," I'd said then, but Michael had never liked being helpless.

Now, his hands tightened into fists. "You told me he wasn't a vegetable."

"I did. But he isn't the same person. He's somebody else."

"Nonsense." Michael stormed past me, clearly determined to find Ben's room himself since I hadn't taken him there.

"Ben isn't there," I said, too softly for Michael to hear. The biggest proof so far that someone else inhabited my son's body was that the person inside had said he was looking forward to seeing his father.

Ben has always loved to draw. Before the shooting, he drew peaceful places, clearings in forests, a grassy river bank, a landscape overlooking a valley towards mountains in the distance. Sometimes there were human figures in the pictures, but rarely, and when they were present, they were faint, hard to discern among the trees and water. I suppose these drawings were the only calm places Ben could find in those days of gangs and graffiti and guns.

Drawing books and pencils were the first things he asked for in hospital, once he'd recovered enough to sit up and use his hands. I'd wondered if it was a good idea to bring him art supplies, since his vision was blurred and the doctor told me it was unlikely to improve. I was glad, though, to find this connection to the old Ben, and did as he asked.

His fine motor control wasn't back to normal, still isn't, but he bit his lower lip and clenched his fingers around a pencil and pushed it across paper. He still draws outdoor scenes of lakes and fields, but they're different now. Out of focus, especially the backgrounds. Almost impressionistic. A piece of heavy machinery dominates each scene. A huge tractor rests by the side of a stream that winds down from a grassy hill. A bulldozer sits in the shallow water by the shore of a wide lake. A train engine sends smoke into the air as it puffs along a root-entwined forest trail. Each is placed in its gentle setting with dark pencil strokes that cut into the paper.

Ben was sitting up in his bed. A drawing book rested against his knees, his forehead was furled in concentration. As Michael entered, he looked up and smiled. "Hello, Father," he said.

For a moment Michael was silent, his mouth working but no words coming out. Then he sat gingerly on the edge of the bed, as if afraid he'd break something. He reached out, more gently than I'd ever seen before, to touch his son's cheek.

"You used to call me Dad," he said, and shut his eyes a moment, as if that wasn't what he meant to say.

"Did I?" Ben asked. "I don't remember." He touched his father's cheek, and for a moment they were connected by the graceful arcs of arms, each extended one to the other. "I remember you, though."

Michael lowered his hand to the edge of Ben's drawing book. "Can I see what you're doing?"

Ben tilted the pad towards him, revealing a semi, cab and trailer, suspended from tree branches in a leafy forest glade.

"Can you tell me about it?" Michael asked. I was surprised. So many times in the past I suggested to him that "What is that? It doesn't look like anything" was not the best thing to say to a child who loved paper and crayons. But Michael had never changed anything he did during the years we'd been together.

"Sure," Ben said. "The machines are all lost. They're in a place where they don't belong. But big machines are strong. People always know when one's around. They pay attention to it. So the machines can never be out of place."

I hadn't asked Ben about his drawings since his injury, not wanting to invade what had always been his private haven. My fingernails bit into my palms. I'd come in here to make sure Michael didn't hurt Ben even more than he already had. But who was there to protect me? My throat tightened and acidic tears filled my eyes. I blinked them back, using what seemed like every muscle in my body to do so.

Michael brushed Ben's limp dark hair from his forehead. "I don't want to tire you. I'll go settle in to my hotel. But I'll be back real soon. Okay?"

Ben nodded. "It's okay, you know." Michael stood, but then froze when Ben added, "That you went away."

I gasped. How can it be okay?

"You were angry," Ben said. "At her." He jerked his chin at me. "I was angry, too. I didn't like it but I was." He paused and his eyes drifted towards his drawing. "I'm not angry now."

"What are you now, honey?" I asked, trying not to weep.

He looked at me, his eyes dark and deep. "I don't know," he said, and returned to his drawing.

The tears were back, and this time I couldn't prevent all of them from escaping. A few ran down my cheek into the corner of my mouth, and I tasted salt.

ഇഇഇ

Michael left. One good thing about the apartment — it was too small for him to stay with us. While he was gone, I made supper for Ben and me, three-cheese macaroni and a spinach salad. I helped Ben out of bed, brought him to the kitchen table, and we ate in silence. He ate everything and then went into the living room to watch *Star Trek*. Before leaving the kitchen, he'd thanked me. That was something else new. He'd never thanked me for anything after Michael left, acted only as if anything I did was the least I owed him. He also never used to eat salad, calling it cow food, looking at me to make sure I knew just who the cow was.

Before, his hate filled the air between us with howls. He blamed me for the loss of his father. How could he not? I blamed me, too.

I raced about the apartment while Michael was gone, picking up magazines and the medical and neurological journals I'd brought home from the lab where I work, and cramming them onto the already full magazine shelf under the coffee table. I washed dishes and dried them, and put them away. I finally forced myself to stop when I found myself plugging in the vacuum cleaner.

Ben was back in his room. He needed a lot of sleep, and often went to bed early. I sank onto the couch, the vacuum cord still entwined between my fingers. I closed my eyes and longed for the central vac I'd installed in my house, and for the dishwasher I no longer had. "Alison," I said out loud. "You're in pretty bad shape if you're nostalgic about housecleaning."

I shut my eyes and remembered the floor between my childhood bedroom and the bathroom, the narrow walnut planks, the place where one nail kept lifting and I had the pleasure of banging it back in with a hammer. And it was a pleasure, the knowledge that the house and I looked after each other. How was it faring now, without me?

The image of the crying woman came to me. I'd been unable to stop thinking of her, while cooking dinner, while eating with Ben, while cleaning. What was the grief so strong she had to clamp it deep inside herself lest it escape, and in doing so, tear her apart?

Suddenly, I'm with her in the house. In the kitchen, where she sits at a glass and chrome table, which does not go at all with my terracotta tile floor and the oak cupboards. She wraps her fingers around a mug of gently steaming tea, and stares at the man sitting across from her. His dark hair is streaked with grey and the lines in his face are deep.

"Are you all right?" he asks. The scent of jasmine, from her tea, is gentle in the air.

"Of course not," she replies, but she doesn't snap the words, merely drones them as if she has no energy for any emotion, least of all exasperation.

He nods. "I'm sorry. It was a stupid thing to say."

She lifts her shoulders, lets them drop, looks down at her tea. He lifts a hand as if to touch her, then stands and goes to the kettle to pour more water into the teapot. Her mug is still full.

"I'm not very good company." She tries a smile as he sits again, a twist of her mouth that looks ghastly.

"I didn't come here to be entertained," he says. "I wanted to see for myself how you are."

Her face goes blank. "I am as you see me. Nothing more, nothing less. This is all there is."

He shakes his head. "No. Maybe you feel that way now, but I know the creativity is still inside."

"No." Her voice cracks across his words, and they both look surprised at its power. "No," she repeats. "This is all I am. A brittle shell, holding nothing at all. An empty husk that will blow away at the first wind."

"I don't like to think of you all alone here, so far away." He holds up his hand. "Don't worry, I know you don't want any of us to stay with you, but the offer still stands. Any time you need us." His voice trails off. She doesn't look at him, stares now out the window over the sink. He adds, gently, "You can't go on this way."

She looks outside, perhaps seeing the tree where my tire swing hung, where I used to pretend I could swing myself right up and over my house, passing by the moon with each arc.

"Do you think I haven't thought that?" She isn't looking at him, couldn't know the alarm that fills his eyes, but says anyway, "Oh, don't worry. I'm not going to kill myself. I'm empty enough for the idea of nothingness to hold little appeal. And besides, doing that would be the act of a coward."

"And you're not a coward," he says, and at this she does look at him. "You know the gallery will always give you space." She starts shaking her head, more and more violently, but he presses on. "When you have more — "

"Everything inside me," she says, her voice so faint a breeze could carry it away, "including where art comes from, turned to ash when Ryan and the dogs died because of my work. Because of me."

They sit silently for a time. "Is there anything I can do?" he asks.

She takes in a deep breath, lets it sigh out as her shoulders slump. "You have helped. By not telling me not to blame myself." She stands, paces from the stove to the door that leads to the front hall, and back, then slams her fist on the fridge door. Something inside rocks, falls, rolls. "Ryan wouldn't have gone to the studio if we hadn't had that fight. He wouldn't have taken the dogs if he hadn't been trying to give me some silence." She forces open her fist, rubs the cold almond enamel. "Silence. It's all I have."

Their voices fade and I become aware of my house's sounds, a creak overhead, the wind sighing outside, a groan as something settles into the approaching cool of night. The man stands, goes to the front door, looks back a moment, then leaves.

The woman sits for a while, stares into her mug, then runs a hand through her short curly hair. She goes to the sink, empties her untouched tea into it, rinses the mug, dries it with a tea towel printed with yellow and pink flowers. The woman leans against the sink, rocks from her hips, her shoulders swaying forward and back as she watches the sky flow from blue to purple to grey.

I drift through the ceiling to the floor above as it creaks again. I visit Ben's room on the top half-story, with its slanting walls. Ben loved being tucked under the eaves. When he was little, he told me he liked his room because the house tucked him into itself just as I tucked him into his bed. There's a water stain now, on the north-facing wall.

The man returns, lets himself in, hands her a plastic bag that hangs heavily from its handles. She moves to the table, pulls out a hammer, three screwdrivers, a pair of pliers, and a bag of nails, and lays them in a row on the table.

"Build," says the man.

"Repair," she says. She opens her arms to him but as he enfolds her against him, her lips tremble.

ꟷꟷꟷ

When I got back to the apartment, Michael hadn't yet returned. I put away the vacuum and had a shower.

I went into the living room, my skin soft from the steam, and found Michael and Ben sharing the newspaper. Ben was reading the front section, not the comics, possibly the first time he had ever done so. They both looked up at me and smiled the same smile, one that pulled back the corners of the upper lip. Why had I never seen before how much they looked alike? Michael finished the business section and handed it to me as I joined them.

"I thought you went to bed," I said to Ben.

"I was drawing," he said.

"He came out," Michael said, "to keep his old man company." Their eyes met for a moment, but I couldn't tell what passed between them, before Ben stood and returned to his room.

Michael leaned back, his hands behind his head, and stretched his legs out. He'd taken the most comfortable chair in the apartment, my old blue recliner.

"You look good." He stood and moved in front of me. "Smell good, too." He lowered his head and nuzzled my neck.

I jerked away. "What are you doing?"

Michael scowled and moved against me again. This time he cupped his hand around the back of my neck, so I couldn't easily move away. "I want my family back." And then, as if realizing that wasn't the most romantic thing he could have said, he added, "I want you back."

"Why?" It was the only thing I could think of to say.

"We were good together." He pulled my head against his chest and brushed his cheek against my hair.

For a moment I relaxed against the hard wall of his chest and the steady thump of his heart. I ducked out of his hold. "We were. When you had time for it."

He sighed. "I know I wasn't always the best husband. But I was working hard to establish myself."

"But we needed you, too." I turned, wanting to get away, be anywhere but here, but remembered that this was my apartment. I would not run away as I did so many times in the past. Then all thoughts of getting away rushed from my head as he said, "Ben thinks it would help his recovery if he had both parents around."

I spun to face him. "You talked to Ben about this? Don't you think he has enough to deal with without feeling responsible for his parents' relationship?"

"Don't you see how our getting back together will be good for him?"

"No. All I see is how hurt he was when you left, when you missed his birthdays, when you never called."

"I want to make it up to you. Both of you. You two can move to the coast. I can help you find a job. You don't have to live with me at first. Won't you give me another chance?"

"I won't let him be hurt again."

"In case you didn't notice, he has been hurt again and while in your custody. He has brain damage, for Christ's sake."

I opened my mouth to respond, but nothing came out. I sank down, reached for the couch to catch myself, but it was too far away and I ended up on the floor, cross-legged.

I heard nothing for a moment, then felt his warmth as he sat beside me. "Do you think I haven't tried?" I whispered.

"I'm sorry." He wrapped his arm around me, pulled me against his shoulder. I stayed tense, refusing to relax into his warmth. "That was a lousy thing to say. I know he was angry. At both of us."

"But only I was there. Do you have any idea how unfair that is?"

We sat in silence, on the beige rug with dark brown diamonds that I got at Walmart after moving here. I ran my fingers along the diagonal lines.

"Please," he said. I felt his breath, hot against my ear. "I've missed you. It will be different this time. Better. I've changed."

I lifted my head. "People don't change that much," I said bitterly.

For a moment, all was still. Then, as one, our two heads turned to look towards Ben's room.

Michael left. I was still down on the rug, and I unfolded and lay on my back. The ceiling spread above me, white and peaceful. I thought about walls, the walls that held up that ceiling, the walls that surround us, those we choose and those we don't.

It had felt good to be held. Warm and safe. And yes, for a moment, loved. But our marriage's walls had held doors only for Michael. I had windows, but they showed me the inside of my house as often as they did the outside world.

The ceiling was stippled in small spirals. My eyes followed the curls. Round and round. In to the centre and back out. The white changes, shifts orientation, becomes a wall. I am standing in the front room in my house. There's a fireplace along one side and big windows facing the street. The windows' outer edges are stained glass, and they hold prismed diamonds, so that in the late afternoon, the room was always filled with rainbows.

There are no coloured lights now. It's night, and the room is dark, lit only by one reading lamp spilling light onto the central angle of a white leather modular sofa. The woman is in the bend where two couch sections meet at right angles. She's wearing faded jeans and a fire-engine red sweatshirt. I drift behind her to look at the book lying in her lap. It's about how to maintain old homes. She turns a page, pauses to examine a diagram that shows the structure behind a lath and plaster wall.

The room is almost empty. There's a light blue rug on the floor, and a couple of chairs against the far wall, but they're lost in shadow. Empty bookshelves line the wall behind the sofa, and cardboard boxes are stacked in front of them. From where I float, behind the lamp, anything outside of the windows is lost in the night. All I see is reflection, the lamp, the sofa, the woman. And myself, behind them all.

A car approaches on the street outside, engine muttering. Its headlights fill the window, chasing away the reflection. A square of yellow light is cast upon the empty wall beside us. It moves across the wall, slowly at first, speeding up as the rumble of tires on concrete and engine sounds increase to a roar. The light flies across the wall, and then is gone.

The reflection is back. In the window, I am smiling. She is teaching herself how to fix my house. I want to touch the woman's hair, but stop before I do, my hand hovering just above her head. She turns another page.

ຄຄຄ

"Mom?"

I opened my eyes. The ceiling shone moon-white over me, while the spirals glowed like stars. Ben's face floated in this pale cosmos.

He knelt beside me. "Are you okay?"

I sat up, cupped my hand around his jaw. "I'm fine. I just discovered that it can be very peaceful lying on the floor."

"Mom?"

"Yes?"

"Is my father going to be living with us again?"

I shake my head. "No. Is that all right?"

He thought for a moment, then nodded. "You know, I'm not sure I do remember him. Maybe all I remember is the idea of him."

I didn't know what to say so I reached out and held him close.

"I'm lonely sometimes," he said. "I can't even be with myself, since I don't know who that is. But I do know that whoever I used to be, you were part of it."

I blinked several times. "I'll always be part of you, whoever you are. Just as you'll always be a part of me."

He picked up a piece of paper from the couch. "I made you a drawing." It's a picture of a jumbo jet taxiing up a mountain trail. We looked at it together. "Soon, he said, "it will reach the top."

"It's beautiful," I said. "Thank you."

He stood. "I guess I'll go to bed, now." He rubbed his right temple.

"Is your head hurting?" I asked, moving so he could slip an arm around my shoulders for balance as we walked.

"It's not too bad," Ben said. I left him while he changed and then came back in his room as he eased himself into bed.

"Mom," he said, and for a moment he sounded like the boy he'd been, when he was little and still had two parents. "This may sound silly but," he paused, "would you tuck me into bed?"

Our eyes met as a big goofy grin spread across my face. I wiped it away and said, "Of course," in a calm voice that suggested he asked such things all the time. I pushed the sheet and blanket under the side of the mattress and smoothed them over his chest.

"Do you remember," he asked, "my room under the eaves in our house?"

"I do." I stood still, my hand still on the covers. Distantly, through the them, I could feel his heart beat.

"I really loved that room."

"I know."

"Do you miss our house?"

I nodded.

He looked away at that, and something about the tightness in his jaw made me realize what he was really asking.

"Oh honey, I don't for a moment blame you for us having to sell it." He looked back at me, his face so young and vulnerable that I had to stop and swallow before I could go on. "Life is full of changes, but what's most important is the people we love. You are more important to me than the house."

"Even though I'm not who I was before? I don't remember much, but — "

I put my arms around his thin shoulders and hold him close. "Mom," he says. "Will you tuck me in every night? Just for a while? I don't know who I am but people are who they are because they were younger once and then they grow into who they are. Maybe I need to be little again."

I nod. "Ben, feel free to grow into whoever you want to be." We hold each other, and over our heads the walls shift, slanting towards the middle of the ceiling, tucking us in close.

The Sand Dove

The last I saw of my husband was his hand sticking out the attic kitchen window. The fingers were spread wide, and I thought I saw a flutter, so maybe he was waving goodbye. Later I realized he couldn't have been saying goodbye because he didn't know I was leaving. I didn't know it myself. I thought I was going to the store to get a can of soup and some noodles for supper.

Instead, I'm here. I drove north a long way and then came to this lake. I walk along the beach and notice small things, things I never had a chance to notice before, what with the TV yapping, cigarette smoke twisting against the ceiling, the click-hiss of a beer can opening, and the smell of slime and blood I brought home from work, no matter how many times I washed up.

Now I see dragonflies. Some are blue, the smaller ones are brightest, a blue so clean it looks electric. If I could see electricity, it would be blue like those dragonflies.

I hear the waves lapping at the sand, and loons crying. Maybe the power boats scare them. I see reeds rising from the water, parallel lines, although they bend, and they wave with the water.

As I walk, I kick up little puffs of sand that fly ahead of me. Sand is made from rocks, and rocks are heavy, but sand can fly anyway. Up ahead is a dark bump, maybe a rock that can't fly, but when I get closer, I see it's a bird.

It tries to flap its wings. It must be heavier than sand, because it can't fly. An oil leak from a power boat, I think, and carry it back to my cabin.

The rent here is really cheap. After I drove past the store and realized I wasn't going to make supper after all, I went to the bank. I'd just got paid, and I took out all the money in my account, that pay and the rest I'd started saving, long ago, when I thought Dave and I would have kids. I kept saving it, never touched it, because taking it out would mean I knew I'd never have a baby.

The cabin is small, just one room, but that's okay, I don't take up much space. I put the bird in the sink. It has dark eyes, and I realize that while I've seen millions of bird eyes, I've seen very few that could look back at me.

It's supposed to be hard to clean oil or whatever off a bird, and I get my toothbrush because once I saw someone on TV cleaning up after an oil spill, and she used a toothbrush to clean a penguin. But when I start cleaning, there is no gooey, tarry stuff. This bird is covered in sand.

Lots of sand, all through its feathers and covering its toes. I run water and comb the feathers with my toothbrush. The bird sits without moving as I try to brush sand from under its wings, and its eyes never leave my face. The sink, a shiny enamel one, fills with mud like the wet sand at the place where the waves come up on the shore. I empty the sink and rinse it three times before I'm done.

I wrap the bird in a clean dish towel and put him under the only table lamp here, so he won't get cold. I sit in the padded chair beside the lamp and watch him.

I worked in the chicken processing plant. Most people in our town do, although Dave has a different job, he's janitor at the school. He tells me about some of the things he's had to clean up, and he thinks his job is worse than mine, but at least there's life in the school, kids running and shouting to each other. I see only dead birds, one after another hanging from the chain, moving past me so fast I can hardly keep up. They're alive when they come in the plant, and I went to see them once, but I couldn't bear it, all those birds crammed together. They were alive and soon they'd be dead, turned into pieces wrapped in plastic.

My bird's alive. His feathers are white, and he's slim with a small beak. I know he's a dove because of a show I saw on the Discovery channel. He lies quietly, nestling into the towel. He's happy, I think, and suddenly I am, too.

I almost don't recognize happiness. I remember the first time I got pregnant, but that joy is thin and shadowy, a memory that must have happened to someone else. The miscarriage, and the next pregnancy, this one lasting into the fourth month, and the next and the next. I couldn't do it any more, hoping, and then only death coming out of me. Oh, but I wanted a baby. Someone to hold, to love, to play with. Dave's a good man, and he loved me, I know, but after the miscarriages he looked for welding jobs on the weekends and I started at the plant. There's not much play in our lives. It's as if we needed a baby to belong together, and without one we live separate lives.

The next morning the bird is gone, but lying on the orange plaid couch, covered with the towel, is a baby. He smiles when he sees me and holds out his arms to be picked up.

I go all-over faint, and sit down on the bed. Birds turning into babies only happens in stories and my life is no fairytale. I did see it happen once, though, when I was eight. Aunt Emma, the aunt my father used to make fun of because she worked in a library, took me to a ballet. I saw the people on stage, they were real, and sometimes the women, so beautiful, were women and sometimes they were swans. As a child, I wanted to believe it was true. Do I know any better now? I stand up and cross the small space between the bed and the couch.

The baby smiles at me, and kicks his legs in the air. I wonder if he's dangerous. The lovely swans killed the prince, after all, even though he kind of deserved it. Do I deserve death, death in the form of four dead babies? This baby's the most alive thing I've ever seen, and I can't help it, I pick him up.

He looks about seven months old. He snuggles into my body, his bare bottom on my arm and tucks his velvety head into my neck just below my chin. I melt. I am flooded with warmth and my head fills with fluttering wings and my heart throbs so hard I have to sit down. The baby looks at me, his expression serious. I look down at him, into his dark eyes. Didn't I hear somewhere that all babies have blue eyes? It doesn't matter, he's perfect just the way he is. I fall into his eyes, deeper and deeper, my finger brushes his feather-soft cheek, and my arms tighten about him.

I'm scared then, and I get up and shut the curtains, even though I've always left them open, even at night. What if someone sees me with him and takes him away? How did he get here, does he belong to someone else? I look into his eyes again and I know he is mine and I am his. We belong together.

Later, when I've made him a diaper out of a dish towel and wrapped another around his little chest like a toga, I head for the store and buy the things he'll need. I carry him with my left arm and with my right I pick up diapers and some baby cream, but when I reach for the cans of formula, he wriggles against me and I feel a hot almost-pain in my nipples, and I look down and see a wet stain spreading across my green T-shirt. I close my eyes and the joy washes through me and I sway where I stand.

Someone puts a hand on my shoulder and asks if I'm okay, and without opening my eyes I tell her I'm more okay than I ever thought I could be. She stands beside me for a moment without moving, and I can tell she's looking at me, so I quickly look at her and smile.

She's younger than me, with unlined skin and dark curly hair. "It's good to see someone so happy," she says, and pushes her cart down the aisle towards the feminine protection products.

When I get back to the cabin I make a nest for him on my bed, frame it with pillows so I won't roll on him during the night. No one comes looking for him, no one knocks on my door although I jump every time I hear feet brushing sand or voices raised in play.

I get into bed beside the baby, but I can't sleep and I reach out to touch him but he isn't there. I sit up, my breath caught in my throat. He hasn't fallen off the bed, and I don't find him anywhere. In the window, the dove turns from where he stares out at the night, looks at me a moment, looks back into the dark.

I pay for another few nights in the cabin, using up almost all the money I have left. During the day I take the baby for walks, and dangle his feet in the waves while he shrieks with joy. His mouth tugs on my nipple and I've never felt so connected to the world. At night, though, the dove sits at the window, yearning. I leave the window open, but I don't think he ever goes out to fly with the stars, because whenever I wake up, which is often, he's there, sitting on the sill, looking out.

I have to wash the dove once a week, because his feathers fill with sand. I thought this meant he must go outside sometimes, so I stayed up all night one time. He never left the sill, but in the morning his white feathers were darker.

This scares me, but the baby is always the same, eager to greet me each morning. He laughs a lot, and is filled with wonder by the smallest things, a tiny crayfish scuttling across the sand, the cry of a gull overhead, a streamer of green weed clutched in his fist. My life is filled with wonder, too. I see how the crayfish holds his claws in readiness, hear the strength in the gull's cry, know by touch of the many miles the weed has floated since it left its deep bed and the company of others like itself.

I wash the dove again, get a new toothbrush. Even with the sand, he is so light. I hold him in my hand and I hold only the weight of a dream. The sand spins in a whirlpool in the bottom of the sink.

When I'm done, and the dove's feathers are again as white as the stars shining outside, I wrap him in his towel, leave him under the lamp, and go outside. The moon makes everything bright. The water is luminous, the sand glows with a pale light. I kick the sand, see it fly ahead of me, but then it settles again onto the beach. I swing my leg back, kick hard; I scoop sand so it covers the top of my foot and then fling it.

I go inside. The dove has struggled free of the towel and sits on the window sill. He doesn't move, looks out instead to where I stand indoors. Already, a light dusting of grains coats his wing feathers. I stand beside him and stare outside, too.

The world is so very big, I think. I had a little piece of it. It makes me sad to think of our little house, and I miss some things about Dave, the times he made me laugh, the soft touch of his rough hands on my skin, his joy when he spoke of the kids at the school who liked him, who actually liked hanging out with the janitor. He belongs in that school. I never belonged in the chicken packing plant and, after the miscarriages, I stopped belonging with Dave.

I cup my hand around the dove, and his feathers caress my palm. I think of the baby, my baby, and my arms long to hold him one more time, my mouth to stretch again in response to his smile, but he doesn't belong to me.

I pick the dove up and take him outside. In the moonlight, the sand is very pale. I scoop some onto my foot and kick it ahead of me. It flies.

"See?" I say. "Sand can fly. Not far, but it flies."

I dig one foot into the sand, to make a footprint, and step ahead to make another. I put the dove down beside my first track.

He stands in the sand, small and white but, as I turn back to the cabin, he takes a hop into the air and spreads his wings.

ഀഀഀ

I'm afraid to phone Dave and tell him I won't be coming home, although he must have guessed by now. I called him when I first came here to let him know I was fine, but I didn't tell him where I was. I spend days, long lonely days, walking and looking for all the things that would have made the baby smile. I find them, too, the silver grey of driftwood and the patterns of its grain. The calls of geese as they fly overhead, heading to a place some have never seen but where they know they belong. The colours of the leaves as they change because the nights are growing colder. The curves and twirls they do as they fall to the ground. They are dying, and still they dance.

I can't go home, to a place where I don't belong. I'm not sure where I do, but being here is a first step to finding it.

I call Dave. "I'm sorry," I say.

"I'll be okay," he says. "You know, I expected this."

And when we hang up, I realize he did. That flutter I saw, the day I left. He wasn't waving. He'd found a butterfly inside, caught it, and released it.

I move out of my cabin, but don't go far. I met a woman who runs a shelter for abandoned pets. There are lots here, she tells me, especially now at the end of the summer. People get dogs, cats, rabbits, all sorts of animals, keep them while they're at their summer place, then don't want them when they return to the city. The pets are left alone at the side of the highway to watch the only world they know drive away. She finds them, or people bring them to her. She has too many to look after, and so I help her. She has no money to pay me, but she gives me a room in her house, food to eat, and the animals to love. I work weekends at the little grocery store, and most of the money goes to the animals.

I don't have to give birth. I only have to give. I walk every day on the beach, late at night when the animals are snuggled together in sleep. I kick the sand. It doesn't fly far before the earth calls it home, but for a moment, the pieces of rock do fly.

Drifting Snow

CALLA BLEW HER NOSE as she walked into the shelter of her apartment building. Cold always made her nose run, and cold combined with wind made it worse.

It was good to be home, her body tired but vibrant after the workout of class. She pulled her scarf away from her face, the wet part where she'd been breathing into it already softening from ice to moist wool in the warmth of the lobby. Before heading for the stairs to climb to her third floor apartment, she checked her mailbox.

The letter nestled between a request for money from Greenpeace and the phone bill. A picture of a ballet slipper was printed beside the return address, its long trailing ribbon looped around the street number. Calla's stomach became a lump of ice colder than anything she'd stepped on coming home from the studio.

She ran her fingers over the envelope. Her feet took her up the stairs, but she was unaware because her head was full of swirling snow.

Once in her apartment, she threw the mail on the table. The letter was on top and rising from it was the scent of rosin, the rhythmic pounding of the piano, and the shrill voice of Madame Esther calling out steps. The envelope contained a world, of discipline, repetition, and pain, but also of freedom of motion, of losing herself in the music to become the dance. The envelope contained either the key to that world, or a door slamming shut in her face. She seized it and tore it open.

She loved her apartment, the one small bedroom where she slept, the other large enough for a barre and space to exercise. Brown and green cushions made up most of the furniture in the living room, together with the card table and two folding chairs where she ate her salads and homemade yogurt.

Her home, so warm and welcoming, suddenly grew cold and barren. The snow in her head raged, howled with the force of a blizzard. A voice grew out of the crying of the wind, a voice both brittle and satisfied. "You failed," it gloated. "You failed. There are other companies to audition for, but what's the point? The company whose school accepted you doesn't want you in the corps, so why would anyone else?"

"No reason," she said, the words lost in the hiss of the snow. The walls of her apartment, once so welcoming, now pressed in on her. Envelope and letter fell to the floor. Grabbing her coat, she ran out the door, down the steps, and out into the cold.

Even the city was too small now, the city that held the theatre with its stage facing the ranks of seats, the orchestra pit, the backstage rooms, the wings where dancers waited for their cues, their bodies eager to be unleashed. She ran down the block, slipping on ice, almost falling, to the garage where she parked her car. The car was seldom used; she walked to the studio where she took her dance classes, but a vehicle was useful for grocery shopping and visits to the farm where she'd grown up and where her parents still took pride in fields of golden wheat.

Their world was shaped by windrows and straight furrows. Calla had never accepted those boundaries. Even the horizon, far away as it was on the flat landscape, had been too confining. Only in dance did boundaries lead to endless possibilities.

Tires spinning, she left the garage and took the road that led north out of the city.

All wasted. The pleading with her parents for dance classes, the knowledge that her sister did without a new dress, her father constantly jury-rigging parts for the disker or the combine, since the money wasn't there for replacements. The money went to the dance school. That first audition, people checked her foot's arch, and watched as she lay on her back, soles together, knees out and touching the floor, to see if the ligaments were flexible. She was a machine, potential users checking its parts to see if it was worth buying.

Her mother had driven her into the city twice a week for classes, and then sat with the other mothers, with them but apart. They were city women who didn't bother to speak to someone with mud on her steel-toed boots.

But there was also the pride in her family's eyes when she'd been accepted to the school, and the glow on their faces when they met her backstage after student performances, moving awkwardly through the crowds, but with their heads held high because they had a right to be there.

How could Calla tell them it had all been for nothing?

"You don't have to," the ice and wind voice told her, and Calla pressed harder on the accelerator and tried not to think.

The last buildings fell away behind her, the sudden transition from city to prairie so familiar it usually went unnoticed. Not today, for she'd hoped that reaching the wide spaces, the distant horizon unseen, white sky blending into white fields, would help her escape the sense that her world was closing in on her. But as she drove, her eyes brimmed with the pressure of unshed tears. The space, the sky surging up over her head, the fields spreading as far as she could see, only served to emphasize that the world was a large place, and she, small and insignificant.

She was alone, the road empty, the houses she occasionally passed closed up tight, the lit windows opening on worlds she couldn't enter. Even the road was invisible, the yellow and white lines that marked the lanes covered by drifting snow.

The snow moved across her path, a never-ending flow drifting from the field on one side to the field on the other. Wire fences keeping what was inside the fields safe from the road were powerless to keep out the snow. It drifted only inches above the hidden tarmac, and skimmed the shoulders on either side, so it was impossible to tell where the road ended and the sides, covered with grass, weeds, flowers during the summer, began.

Her world was nothing but white, above, below, to the sides. This must be what it's like in outer space, she thought, no way to tell what's up and what's down. There was gravity here, or so she assumed, for the car speedometer told her she was moving, and her body pressed firmly into the seat. What if the speedometer had decided to play a trick, and showed motion where there was none? There was no way to tell if she was moving or still, even though the drifting snow moved across her path, and she could see wisps and thicker strands in the flow. With everything around her white, there was nothing ahead to move closer to, nothing behind to move away from.

A wave of dizziness swept through her, and the sensation that the car was standing still, floating on a sea of white, was too strong to overcome. This is my life, she thought, and noticed she was clenching the steering wheel hard enough to hurt her fingers. Fuel burned, mechanical parts worked together, just as they should, and for what? The car isn't moving. I am standing still.

But she wasn't in outer space. Forward was forward, and gradually the road ahead of her, arrow-straight behind, slipped into a bend and a gentle descent. The river, wide and placid through the city, twined its body into a braid out here. Snow gleamed against the ice-covered water.

A small park nestled into a bend sharper than most, one strand of the river reaching towards the road before looping back. A bridge spanned the water, leading to a flat island. During the summer, Calla often met her parents or sister here, halfway between the farm and the city, to picnic on the grass.

No grass warmed the park now with cheerful green, but the place still called to her. "Here," the voice rasped, grainy with snow, "here, you will find peace."

She left the car in the small parking lot. There were no car tracks in the snow, no sign that anyone had ever been here. Ice coated the bridge planks, and Calla clutched the railing, her bare fingers, for she'd rushed out of her apartment too quickly to remember gloves and scarf, stiff and ablaze with pain. She tucked her hands into her pockets as she trudged across the open area.

Family picnics had taken her no further than here, people happy to lie on the grass and paddle in the water. Further on, though, beside the river's main stream, trees grew thickly. Not tall trees like she'd seen on trips east and west of the prairie, but trees all the same. Roots, trunk, branches, leaves. No leaves now, of course, but that didn't matter.

It was odd to find a thick cluster of trees here. Few plants other than grasses could grow on the dry and windy prairie. There was water from the river here, and some shelter from the river valley, but why were there no other wooded copses growing between hill and river?

People rarely went close to the trees. They never sat in their shade, even on the hottest days. There was something about them that made people uncomfortable. The shadows were cold, not pleasant, and the rustling leaves joined with the wind to sing, not with joy at the brief summer, but with sorrow for how soon winter would return.

Calla panted, the wind and dry, cold air robbing her of breath. She ran across the flat island, hearing the laughter of her sister and father as they threw a ball back and forth, feeling the sun warm on her skin as she lay back in the grass and watched the clouds float overhead. A gust sent a swirl of snow into her face, the flakes needling her skin. She squinted and ran faster.

Suddenly the wind was gone, the air still and heavy. Dark columns striped the winter grey and white. She'd reached the trees, and even though their leaves were gone and the trunks weren't clustered all that thickly, they were enough to form a windbreak.

The branches reached up, many of the thinner twigs encased in ice. They didn't move, the ice was still and unbroken.

"Poor trees," she said aloud, "to reach endlessly and never attain." Then, *stupid*, she scolded herself. *Don't impose your own world on this one.* She touched a trunk, pulling her fingers away quickly as the rough bark seared her skin with its cold.

A swirl of snow caught her eyes, but when she turned, all was still, twigs unmoving with no wind to push them. The trees weren't towers after all. Most trunks were bent, limbs twisted. Nothing could grow straight in this climate. Ugly things, trying for a life that was doomed before it began.

"You don't belong," she said, her tongue curling around the words. "You," she pointed towards one whose trunk bent at a forty-five degree angle, "look like Annie trying to do an arabesque with her bottom humped up above her leg. And you," this to a tree with branches that flailed in all directions as if hoping that trial and error would find the sun, "are Jeremy, practicing how he'll lift me into a star hold, but no matter what he does, he drops me." Her cheeks stiffened as hot tears transformed into ice.

She spun, pointing at trees all around. "You're Kevin, who left the school when Madame laughed at your pirouettes. You cried then, I saw, even though you tried to hide it. You cried, and you left and you never came back. And you, you're Mary, too fat to jump, but trying anyway, not noticing how the floor shakes when you land. And Diane, with your arms held out so ungracefully, like sticks, how could you ever think — "

"So cruel?" The voice was soft and sibilant, drifting snow scraping on packed snow.

Calla stepped back with a gasp. A woman stood beneath the drooping branches of Diane's tree, but even as Calla watched, the branches lifted, straining away from the woman until they were held out, if not in a perfect second arabesque position, at least in a closer approximation.

The woman stared at Calla, her eyes glittering like chips of ice. Her white hair was very short, hoarfrost clinging to her scalp. "A dancer," she said. "I haven't had a dancer for a long time." Her pale lips stretched into a smile.

A wind swept through the previously silent cluster of trees, swirling around the woman, setting the ice-encased branches to swaying. A few broke, falling with the sound of shattering glass.

Calla didn't move, not even reacting when a branch thicker than most fell with a crash beside her. "Had a dancer?"

"Oh yes." The woman waved her arm, encompassing the trees whose branches now creaked and groaned. "I have them all." Her arm was encased in material as clear and shiny as ice. It covered her body, too, cloudy in places, ice with impurities. It flowed over her as she moved. She laughed, the sound shivering through Calla.

Calla took a step back, her foot slipped and she wavered. She flung her arms up and fell, landing heavily in a sitting position, hurting her tailbone. The worst pain, though, was in her feet. She looked at them, at the end of her sprawled legs. Ice shards of broken branches had sliced into her boots, leaving gaping slits through leather and the wool of her socks. A single drop of blood oozed out one of the cuts, clung for a moment to the edge of the boot sole, then fell to spread, bright red, on the snow.

Calla scrambled up. Her feet were on fire, and her blood seeped out, sinking deep into the ground.

The woman slid across the snow, her face now only inches from Calla's. "Take root." The words slithered across Calla's skin, leaving a trail of ice. "Your world grows small. The walls close in. Stay here, let your bare branches reach for what you could not grasp."

"No." A tree branch twined about her waist. Calla flinched, but instead of pinching tight, the wooden arm pulled, giving her the strength to take a step, then another, away from the woman. "It's winter now, but soon it will be spring. I'll have leaves again someday."

The woman shrugged, the motion sending a cascade of snow flakes from her body to the ground. "Winter, summer, there's no difference. Reach for the sun, cry for the moon, it doesn't matter what you dream. I am always here." Her eyes suddenly flared brilliant white, and Calla cried out, flinging up an arm to protect herself.

The branch jerked against her, whipping free, but others reached down, tugging on her arms, her chest, her neck. Jeremy, she thought. Are you here, your hold so strong now? She turned, her feet slipping, but stayed up with the aid of the trees, took a step, another, and was suddenly running, arms bent to keep falling ice and blowing snow from hitting her face. The wind howled through the trees, or the trees howled within the wind, their voices brittle, but Calla heard only sorrow for what might have been. The woman's laughter followed her, driving up swirls of snow that twined about her.

She was suddenly out of the trees, running across the island, feet slipping, arms flailing to keep her balance. Glancing back she saw no sign of pursuit, nothing but the flat snow-covered expanse, her line of bloody footprints the only evidence that anyone had ever been there.

She used her hands on the bridge railing to pull herself along, her breath now coming in short hot bursts, ice burning her fingers. She bumped into her car with a thump, gasping, heart pounding, and rested against it for a moment before jerking the door open and falling into the driver's seat.

She backed up, tires crunching the snow, back end fishtailing, and roared onto the highway. The river flowed away behind her, the valley rising to flat fields that spread to either side. White everywhere she looked, drifting snow blowing across the road, skimming ditches, covering the black tarmac and lane markings. It looked as if she was standing still, no way to tell she moved, nothing to see coming towards her, nothing to look back at and see shrinking away in the distance. It looked as if she stood still, but she knew she moved forward.

Death TV

On the screen a man, wrinkled face peaceful, rolled his eyes towards the camera, and breathed his last. Perry reached for another handful of potato chips and munched on them, watching as the show switched to another deathbed scene. In this one, grieving relatives surrounded the dying woman's hospital bed, but the camera zoomed in on her face, ignoring those who loved her. This was her death, her moment in the spotlight.

Peter, seated on the next bar stool to Perry, nudged him. "She reminds me of your last girlfriend's dog. What was it, a poodle?"

"A Pekingese," Perry said without moving his eyes from the wall screen.

The woman's death was more difficult than the previous one shown on *Hospital Hush.* Several times she stopped breathing, only to cough or make choking sounds. Her cheeks turned red, then blue. She coughed again, shiny spittle running down her chin. Fear pulsed in her pain-blurred eyes, and she glanced from time to time at the camera for reassurance.

Perry finished his chips, salt stinging his lips, and reached for his beer.

The camera pulled back a bit, showing hands which held hers, smoothed the blanket across her chest, stroked her hair. She shook them away, her gaze now firm on the camera, and started to smile but a cough deeper than the rest shook her thin frame. A stream of red blood joined the saliva on her chin; she convulsed, arching up from the bed, and collapsed back into stillness.

Abruptly, the show went to a commercial. Perry wondered for a moment, since usually the image lingered on the dead person, then realized one of the grieving relatives must have thrust his or her face in front of the camera, hoping to achieve that highest of aspirations, a moment on TV. The producer had cut the shot at that point, rightfully leaving the viewers' focus on what they tuned in every week to see — the dying becoming the dead.

Perry drained his beer and Peter lifted two fingers, signalling the bartender. "How long," Peter asked, "do you think they have to keep the camera rolling before the people kick off? Doesn't it get expensive to record so much time of people lying there ready to die?"

He hadn't asked this specifically of Perry but everyone turned to him anyway. Perry was the acknowledged expert on anything to do with the Death TV network. They all wanted to be on one of the shows, of course, but he was the only person they knew who would be, and he didn't have to die to do it. He'd had his home-video cube accepted by the most popular show of all, Siren Call.

"The cameramen develop an instinct," he told the gang at the bar, "and the doctors and nurses help. But they'll run camera for as long as it takes. Death TV is devoted to its viewers, and no expense is too great to bring the best shows possible to the people."

"Man, listen to you," Joe, three stools down, crowed. "No wonder they're having your cube on the show. You sure know the network line."

"Shut up." Peter reached over and punched Joe on the shoulder. "You're just jealous. Perry worked damn hard for his success and he deserves it."

Perry's eyes were still on the TV, which now showed a young man dying from injuries suffered in a motorcycle accident. He knew this guy, he realized with a sudden thrill. He'd heard the call for an ambulance go out over the radio, had rushed to the scene of the accident hoping to shoot a death. It had looked at the time as if the victim might pull through. But even though Perry, and the young man, lost that chance to achieve immortality on Death TV, here the motorcyclist was, sharing his death with millions of viewers. And here Perry was, having found another death scene, bloodier and more dramatic, about to achieve his lifelong goal. He watched the young man die, feeling a bond more intimate than anything he'd shared with the girl who'd owned the Pekingese, and smiled.

ฉฉฉ

Raymond Baines unscrewed the lid of one of the glass jars and carefully lifted the twig from inside it. Hanging from the twig was a green chrysalis, its surface shiny with horizontal ridges near the top and brown spots near the bottom. "You're just about ready, my beauty," he said. He put the twig back, checked the lid to make sure the air holes were clear, and surveyed the row of gleaming jars which rested on the mantelpiece.

With regret he turned away and puttered about his tiny apartment, throwing back curtains to allow the morning light entry, and watering his African violets. Noticing a dead leaf on one of his geraniums, he pinched it off and placed it in the compost bucket.

"You're all just about ready," he said to the jars, "and I'm ready to go to work. Don't come out yet. Wait for me."

He picked up his long black coat and the top hat he had to wear when he was in public areas at work at the Misty Path Funeral Home. A knock at his door startled him, and he dropped the hat. It rolled under the kitchen table. He bumped a table leg when he crawled to retrieve it, and the potted plants on the tabletop trembled, their leaves rustling. The knock came again.

Raymond backed out from under the table, hat clutched in one hand. He leaned over the plants. "So sorry to disturb you." His finger lingered on a hyacinth leaf, caressing, then he straightened and went to the door.

A woman, dressed in a pink blazer and white skirt, smiled at him. "Good morning. Do I have the honour of addressing Mr. R. Baines?" From behind her, a video camera strapped to the wrist of a lanky young man stared unblinkingly at Raymond. He turned his face away, his stomach suddenly in knots.

"I'm not buying anything." He hoped he sounded like somebody who merely resented the interruption. He also hoped he sounded firm, because the last time a salesperson had come to his door he'd bought seven all-purpose can openers. He'd constructed a bird perch out of them. It stood in his backyard, and was especially favored by wrens, but he was determined not to buy anything today.

"I'm not selling anything." She pushed past him, the cameraman following behind her. "I'm here to offer you the opportunity you've always dreamed of."

Raymond ran his fingers along his hat brim. "I'm just on my way out."

The woman glanced about his room. "I'm Tina Remko, an associate producer with Death TV." She paused, her hands outstretched.

He stood at the still-open door. Would it look suspicious if he just bolted outside? "I have to — "

Her eyebrows lifted. "You aren't excited about why I'm here?"

Maybe her visit was innocent. He glanced hesitantly at the camera. It made a whirring sound, not unlike that of a cicada. "I don't own a TV."

Her eyes widened. She looked about his room as if hoping to find a set hidden in a shadowy corner. She spotted the jars on the mantel and ran her fingertips along their lids.

"I'm sorry," he said, and was immediately angry at himself for apologizing. "Please be careful of the jars."

"Oh I will." She smiled, showing very white teeth. "They're the reason I'm here. You're the reason I'm here."

"I don't understand."

She stepped forward and took his hand, pulling him until he sat beside her on the sofa. "Are you truly unfamiliar with Death TV?"

The cameraman panned along the row of jars, then crouched facing the sofa. Raymond nodded, looking down at his knees.

She patted his hand. "Don't feel bad. Soon you'll be intimately acquainted with us. Death TV airs the top-rated network shows of all time. *Hospital Hush*, *Executioner's Hour,* and *Siren Call* are, respectively, the third, second, and most popular programs there have ever been."

Whatever her reason for being here, it was foolish of him to stay in front of a camera. "I really have to go to work."

"Next week," she said, "we launch the first show of our new series, *Arena*." Again she seemed to be waiting for a reaction from him. When none was forthcoming, she continued. "Surely you've heard of *Gladiators*?"

"People at work talked about it."

"One hundred and thirty-eight million people watched that program. That's more than watched the Superbowl last year, more even than watched the *Celebrities in Court* miniseries."

Raymond tried to stand up, but her hand tightened on his, nails digging into his palm, and he stayed where he was.

"Based on the success of our special, we've developed a regular series. To celebrate and promote its launch, we're running short segments which we're calling *Focus on Life*."

She let go of his hand. He prepared to spring to his feet, but watched her carefully first, massaging his palm. Her nails were awfully long and sharp.

"We want you," she said with an exultant smile, "to be one of our first featured guests on Focus on Life."

Raymond shook his head, slowly at first, then more decisively. "I don't need television. I have butterflies."

"You don't understand. You won't be watching television. You'll be on television, and millions of people will be watching you." She faced the camera and smiled. "One of your co-workers at the Misty Path told us all about you. What he had to say was most interesting. I know our viewers would like to share it."

Raymond swallowed, his mouth suddenly dry. "I don't want to be on TV. I don't want people who watch Death TV to watch me. They watch the shows to see people die. I see people after they've died every day, at work. I put makeup on — "

"And that's precisely why we want you. You work with the dead and you create life."

"I do not create life." Raymond was horrified. "I raise butterflies."

"Most butterflies are extinct." Tina moved to the row of glass jars, ran her fingers along their sides. "And yet here, in your room, they live."

"Please go away. You don't understand." He sidled over to the mantel and tried to push his body between Tina and the jars. "Butterflies mate and lay eggs. I keep the eggs safe. I provide food for the larvae. I keep the pupae safe. When the butterflies emerge, I — "

"Mr. Baines." Tina took his hand. "Raymond. You clearly love your work with the butterflies. It's important work, preserving a soon-to-be-lost-forever species. You must share it with the world."

He shook his head.

"Tell me," she said. "What sort of butterflies are these?"

"*Danaus plexippus.*" He looked at her suspiciously. "Commonly known as monarchs."

"How fascinating," she murmured. "Tell me more."

Ten minutes later she handed him a contract and a pen. He finished telling her about the palpi, the pair of jointed sensory organs found on each side of a butterfly's mouth. She clasped her hands together at her breast and her eyes were big and round. "Masterful," she said. "Sign here." The cameraman zoomed in on the glass jars.

There was a risk, but surely it was outweighed by the opportunity to educate the public about butterflies. Raymond, his head filled with an image of himself teaching hordes of rapt viewers about probosci and compound eyes composed of ommatidia, signed.

ඬඬඬ

The roar of the motorcycle vibrated along Perry's legs and surged up his spine. He drew in a deep breath through the Airomatic, attached by its hose to the O_2 bottle hooked to the bike, and felt the rush brought on by breathing clean air. The bottle was expensive, but without it he wouldn't be able to put in the many hours on his bike. He downshifted, the engine's scream echoing off the boarded windows and dirty brick of a row of buildings, and leaned into a sharp turn, avoiding the blackened husk of a car which lay on its side in the middle of the intersection. He lifted his goggles and sent a sharp glance towards the car. He'd have to come back here and see if there were any useable parts. Wind surged through his hair, sending it streaming in a tangled blond flow back across his shoulders as he picked up speed and roared through the Philly streets.

He could still remember when there was a helmet law, but that was long ago, before he was old enough to ride. New laws left people free to make their own choices, and that was the sign of a civilized society. Perry knew those laws were referred to as Darwin laws, that people said they encouraged the survival of the fittest and most intelligent. Stupid people did stupid things like not wearing helmets, and died in accidents, thus preventing the spread of their stupid genes. Perry knew it was the people who talked like this who were stupid.

The radio pickup in his ear crackled into life, a terse male voice calling a code ten fifty-one. "Action," Perry said resolutely. His video camera was a reassuring weight on his back. The radio voice called for a fire truck as well as an ambulance, and gave the location.

Train crossing, Perry thought. He leaned into a tight U-turn, left foot flat on the cracked pavement, back tire sliding around, and screamed off towards the accident site. He never felt so alive as when he was on his bike, listening in on the police band, racing ambulances. Even though he'd finally achieved his dream and had a cube accepted by Death TV, he wanted more. If he sold more cubes, maybe they'd hire him as a regular cameraman.

He revved up his engine and tore through an area which used to be a park, filled now with stunted trees and dry littered ground. He'd once filmed a drug overdose death here, but the Siren Call producer said ODs were too common. This train-car collision might be paydirt. He had to get there first, beat the ambulance so if anyone was dying he could shoot it in its purity, without the messy interference of CPR and unsightly tubes.

He wasn't far from the train crossing. He roared down Broad Street, weaving in and out between the cars backed up at a red light, zipped through the cross traffic, ignoring the horn blares and curses flung his way, and picked up speed as he turned onto a more deserted road. He felt lucky today. This afternoon was his interview on Death TV. What a coup it would be, an interview and a cube sale on the same day.

Maybe the vehicle hit by the train would be more than just a single car. Maybe it would be a school bus. It was the early morning rush hour, kids would be on their way to school. Children crying, screaming as their guts spilled out and blood streamed into their eyes. Now that would be good TV.

ᏍᏍᏍ

Perry was late for work. He didn't know if it was his bad mood over the disappointing accident scene — the two people in the car had been killed instantly by the collision, the ensuing fire had been easily extinguished by the fire truck which arrived shortly after Perry — but the atmosphere in the garage seemed subdued. The clanking of wrenches and the hiss of the air compressor were as loud as ever, but the guys weren't joking around and even the cars crouched on the grease-slicked floor as if expecting blows instead of repairs.

"Hi guy." Peter raised a hand as Perry pulled on his coverall and walked over to the day's list. "Good hunting?"

"Nah. Same old same old." Perry read the work order for the next car on the list, got its key, and headed outside. He liked his job, liked working on old cars, liked grease and oil and the smell of flammable fuel. Old cars like these were rare now and the owners paid well to keep them running. When he drove into his bay, Peter was waiting for him.

"Jonesy got it last night."

"What?" Perry got out of the car and glanced over to the office at one side of the garage, where Joe Jones usually sat answering calls, writing up work orders, and taking customers' money. A new guy sat there now, someone Perry hadn't seen before.

"There was a war at 3rd and Locust." Peter shrugged. "Joe walked by at the wrong time."

Perry put a hand on the car roof. The blue enamel was pitted with rust. Joe was the third person he knew who'd died in the last two months. One had been Rafe, another mechanic. He'd worked full-time on the fleet of taxis the garage kept running, and had a sideline — putting bags of cocaine in with the air filter which the fleet owner then distributed to his customers. Rafe died in a shootout during a police raid at the taxi office. The other death had been Marie, Perry's cousin who'd been hit on the head by a piece of masonry falling from a building.

Everyone knew people who died. People did die. It happened. It happened a lot.

But not to me, Perry thought. I'm going to be on Death TV and I don't have to die to get there.

"Poor Jonesy," he said out loud. "He never saved enough money to buy that leather jacket. It's still in the store window." He lifted the hood on the blue car and surveyed the engine.

"Yeah." Peter's voice went soft, difficult to hear over the garage sounds. "An empty death. At least if he'd gone out on Death TV it would have meant something."

Perry straightened and stretched his back to relieve a kink.

"Say," Peter said. "Your TV interview is this afternoon, isn't it?"

He said this as if it had just now entered his mind but Perry knew the fact he'd be on Death TV was emblazoned on everyone's minds in fiery gold letters.

"Yeah," he said, and he couldn't keep the excitement out of his voice. "I'm taking off early, gotta get to the studio by four."

As if they were mind readers, the other mechanics drifted over, somehow knowing Death TV was being mentioned.

"Doesn't that new show start this week?" Mike asked. "*Arena*?"

Perry nodded.

"I hear," Peter elbowed him in the ribs, "that some of the gladiators are women."

The others crowded in closer. "No." "Really?" "Will they wear brass bras?" "How do they get chosen to be on the show?"

"All the gladiators," Perry said, "are prisoners. They're given the choice of appearing on *Executioner's Hour* or fighting on *Arena*."

"Man, I know which I'd choose," Peter said.

Perry shrugged and turned back to the blue car. "At least on *Executioner's Hour* it's quick. In the arena, who knows how you'll die."

"Yeah," Mike said, slapping him on the back, "but blood and slow death will rack up the ratings."

Perry slid into the driver's seat. Mike was probably right. But right now *Siren Call* was still the number one show, and that was all he cared about. His cube, his face, on the highest rated show ever.

ꙮꙮꙮ

Perry zipped home to shower before his interview. He scrubbed grease from under his fingernails and slicked his hair back, tying it behind his neck with a leather thong. He put on a clean white T-shirt and black jeans, boots, and his leather jacket.

The roar of his bike echoed off the glass facades of the downtown skyscrapers. He didn't come to this part of the city often; private security and medical personnel were part of every business here. Public ambulances were rarely needed.

He found a place to park only a few blocks away from Death TV. He recognized the building, even though he'd never been here before, as it was part of the Death TV logo. Tall, with thick black beams framing gold glass windows, it widened towards the middle and narrowed to a point at the top. He left his Airomatic and goggles on the bike. He didn't want to look soft.

He entered and drew in a breath of the sweetest, purest air he'd ever inhaled. This building must be sealed, probably used a molecular sieve, too. But when had money ever been a problem for Death TV?

His footsteps were loud on the black marble floor as he approached the receptionist's gold-plated desk. "Sign in, name and show," she said, and he spared only a glance for her long white neck and tight sweater, so proud was he to write the words 'Siren Call' right next to his name in the leather book.

The receptionist pressed a button and a door, one of many leading from the lobby, buzzed. "Down there," she gestured. "You'll find the green room on your left."

His breath tightened in his throat as he pulled the door open and entered the world of Death TV. This was where it all happened, where shows were produced, where freelance cubes were edited into the programs which were seen by millions of viewers. He was part of this world now.

The green room wasn't green and he would have walked right past it if there hadn't been a young woman standing by its door waiting for him. "In here," she said with a smile. "Make yourself comfortable. An associate producer will be by to see you shortly."

An associate producer! Perry still wasn't breathing right, but he smiled at the woman as if he chatted with associate producers every day of his life, and swept through the doorway.

The thick carpet was black, the couches orange and gold. A mirror covered one wall, a screen filled another. The TV showed an ad for UV-protectant lotion. The free walls held slices and Perry recognized the hosts of all his favourite shows, and some images which were from various programs. One showed an executioner, large axe resting on his shoulder. On another was an electric chair, the man strapped to it mugging for the camera and showing a thumbs up sign. Others were of accident scenes and hospital rooms, all the people shown smiling, their expressions peaceful and happy. Of course they were happy, they'd died on Death TV. Perry reached to touch the frame of a car accident scene. Maybe someday a slice from his cube would hang here.

He paced the room, too excited to sit, and then noticed he wasn't alone. A man sat in a corner. He had a thin mustache and short dark hair, and he held a top hat on his lap.

Perry's heart sank. He'd thought he was the only one to be featured on *Siren Call* today.

The man smiled, a tentative stretching of his pursed mouth, and Perry relaxed. No way did this little guy follow the siren call.

"Hi." He sat down on the couch across from the man. "I'm here for *Siren Call*." He said this proudly, and was disappointed to get no reaction. "What show are you here for?"

The man tilted his head. "I'm not exactly sure. I was told I'd be doing a segment for something called *Focus on Life*. It's got to do with the new program. What's it called again? Oh yes, *Arena*."

Despite himself, Perry was impressed. The first of the regular *Arena* series programs was to be broadcast tonight and this man was part of it. The gladiators were probably in the building this very moment.

The little man didn't look very excited, though. He glanced about the room, and Perry got the impression he was looking for escape routes. But then he sat up straight and faced Perry.

"I'm going to talk about butterflies."

Perry wasn't sure he'd heard right. "Butterflies?"

The man held out his hand. "Raymond Baines. I raise butterflies."

Perry shook hands.

"It's a pleasure to meet you," Raymond said. "I raise plants, too. I'm surrounded by death all day, so I foster life in my home. I have seventeen different classes of plants. Only one butterfly species now, though."

"You work with death?" Finally this odd man's presence was beginning to make sense.

Raymond looked down and brushed the side of his hat. "Yes. I'm a mortician's assistant."

An undertaker. As far as Perry knew, there weren't any programs about what happened to people after they died. New shows were pitched all the time to Death TV. A vision of himself as associate producer, or even executive producer, of his own show flashed into his mind. He'd call it *After Death*, no, *After Life*, no, *At The Grave's Edge* . . . well, he'd think of something. "Tell me about your work. It must be fascinating."

Raymond sighed, his thin chest rising and falling. "It's not. I take dead bodies and make them look alive for viewings. People don't want their dead to look dead. I put makeup on faces and dress the bodies in beautiful clothes. The relatives tell me the bodies look asleep, and I smile as if that's a compliment." He sighed again, and looked about in a bewildered way. "I'm sorry to drone on like this. I feel out of place here. I'm really not sure why I came."

"You're not sure?" Perry was amazed. "Most people would die to get on Death TV."

Raymond smiled. "That's precisely what they do, isn't it."

Perry's hands flitted about in the air, grasping for the right words. "But dying on TV gives them immortality. Their death will live forever."

"Or until the cube degrades." Raymond smiled wryly, then his face sobered at the sight of Perry's expression. "Again, I'm sorry. I did a little research into the Death TV programs after I agreed to be on one, and I didn't much like what I saw. But you obviously love them. I shouldn't take that away."

"How can you not like them?"

"I don't have to watch death on TV." Raymond stood up and put his hat on his head. He looked like a mushroom. "I see death in all its forms, violent, peaceful, and everything in between. Brave death and cringing death. Sought-after death and unwelcome death. In the end it's all the same. Life is over."

"But," Perry said, "if the death is on TV, it lives on."

Raymond sat again. "Death can't be alive. Look for immortality some other way, young man. I seek mine on the wings of butterflies."

Perry shook his head, trying to make sense of this. Fortunately he was saved from having to respond by the entry of two women.

One was huge, not fat but heavily muscled. She wore a short skirt made of metal plates and what Perry recognized with a thrill as an armoured bustier. The other woman was small and blonde, wearing white slacks and a pink jacket with a Death TV brooch pinned to the lapel.

"Raymond," the smaller woman said with a smile. "Tina Remko. Remember me? We met at your apartment."

Raymond started to say something, but Tina had already whirled to face Perry. "And you must be today's siren. Welcome. I've seen your cube. It's very impressive."

Perry felt himself redden as he took her small hand in his.

"This is Abigail." Tina gestured towards the big woman. "One of our very first gladiators. She's fighting tonight." She pulled a small notebook out of her jacket pocket and consulted it. "Raymond, your segment will be shot in just a few minutes so you can come with me. Perry, *Siren Call* is in Studio C, and is just getting set up now. In about fifteen or twenty minutes someone will be along to get you. While you wait you can watch Raymond's segment."

Tina and Raymond left, Raymond fussing with his hat, and Perry was alone with the gladiator. He studied her out of the corner of his eye. He thought of himself as well-muscled, but she put him to shame.

She caught him looking at her arms. "I work out a lot," she said. "Lots of spare time in prison."

"What are you in prison for?" he asked without thinking.

She eyed him with a small smile. "Murder. My boyfriend and his floozie."

"Oh." The word squeaked out, and Perry sat up straighter, squaring his shoulders. "Why are you here?"

"They separated the gladiators." Abigail began to pace, her metal skirt clanking. "Someone went a little nuts, and I guess the producers were afraid we'd kill each other before the cameras were ready. So we all got sent to different places." She showed her teeth in a grin and sat beside him. "I guess you got lucky because this is where I'm supposed to wait."

"It's nice to have company." He smiled to show that being alone with a murderer didn't faze him a bit. "But I meant why are you on *Arena*? Do you like fighting?" Ideas for new shows to pitch were popping up all over in his brain. What about one on the urge to kill? *Murderer's Mind*. He could see the opening credits, big black letters dissolving in red drips, and his name right after the show's name, as producer and creator.

"All murderers are condemned to death," she said, her large hands clenching her knees. "Seems like most crimes are capital offenses these days."

"Overpopulation," Perry murmured.

Abigail nodded. "That's the reason they give. No sense in keeping us anti-social types around, using up resources." She looked down for a moment, her jaw clenched, then took in a deep breath and turned back to him. "Some of us, if we're good or photogenic, are given a choice of dying on TV on *Executioner's Hour.* Now we can also choose the arena." Her lip curled. "*Executioner's Hour* is for wimps. And besides, if we're victorious in twenty-five matches, our sentences will be commuted to life in prison." She clenched her hands into fists. "We shot some practice matches when the TV people were deciding if a regular show would work. I was on the special, too. All matches are to the death. I've won six now." She turned her face away.

Perry said nothing. This woman sitting beside him had killed at least eight people. He hesitated to ask his question, but decided real producers let nothing stand between them and good TV. "How does it feel," he asked, "to kill someone?"

Abigail looked at him, then back at her hands, now hanging limply between her knees. "It's better to not feel."

"But," he said, "what about when you — "

She whirled to face him, her eyes flat and hard. "You want to know, do you? You think it would look good on TV, right, for me to spill my guts?" She gestured at the mirror. "There's a camera back there, did you know that?"

Perry hadn't known, but he wasn't surprised.

"They've got something big planned for today," Abigail said, "but me talking isn't it. Not enough drama. But I bet it's enough drama for you." She leaned in closer, and he could feel her hot breath on his face. "You want to know how it feels?"

"Well," he started, but she rushed on.

"It's like acid, eating you inside, etching a hole in your soul that grows each hour, its edges ragged and bloody. My boyfriend was no good, ok? I know that now. I was skinny then, and he knocked me around. I could never fight back.

I was scared. But when I saw him with her, doing what they were doing . . . "

She closed her eyes. "I wish I hadn't done it. I work out in prison, make myself strong, so I'll never again get in a situation where I have to let the anger grow, build up." She opened her eyes, looked at the mirror.

Perry looked, too, at reflections, hers and his, the edges wavy. Was there a darker shadow behind the images, the bulk of a camera?

"And now," Abigail said, her voice quiet, "I'm strong and I kill again and again, not in anger but because it's entertainment. I bet you want to know how that feels, too." She sagged back against the couch.

Perry didn't know what to say. He thought about taking her hand. He who never shrank from shooting the bloodiest, most violent real-life dramas, was afraid of comforting a woman. "I'm sorry," he began. "I — "

"Oh look." She stood up and went to the TV monitor. "It's your friend." She turned up the volume. "There's nothing you can do," she said to the screen, but Perry heard the words. She sat back down beside him and the two of them watched the TV.

On the screen, Raymond sat on a red couch. Behind him was a backdrop showing the silhouettes of trees, branches bare against an orange sky. The camera panned to show the host, a man with red spiky hair.

"Good evening," the host said. "I'm Lorne Buckingham. Welcome to *Focus on Life*. These segments, interspersed with our regular programming, are in honour of our exciting new series, *Arena*, and will focus on that which comes before death — life."

He turned to Raymond and the camera pulled back to show both men. "My guest this evening is Raymond Baines, a mortician who raises butterflies." He smiled at the camera, his eyes saying, "This is a joke, I know, but won't you share it with me?" Perry smiled back.

Lorne Buckingham turned his smile on his guest. "Tell us, Raymond, what is the lifespan of a butterfly?"

Raymond blinked. "Lifespans vary greatly, depending on species. The variegated fritillary, for example — "

"How long do your butterflies live?"

Raymond bowed his head. "Not long. There's so little habitat left, and the pollution in air and water affects them dreadfully. But while they are alive, oh," he looked up, directly at the camera, "I want to tell you about while they are alive."

"Some of our viewers may be interested in collecting butterflies," Lorne cut in smoothly. "How does one kill a specimen? Is it with chloroform?"

Raymond looked bewildered. "One can't collect butterflies these days. So many species are extinct and those that remain are extremely rare. We must breed and release them, not kill them. We must plant flowers and try to — "

"But they're so beautiful, pinned to a board. Such magnificent colours."

The camera was tight on Raymond's face at this point, and a change came over the small man. His brows lowered, his lips tightened. "I prefer to focus on their lives, not their deaths. My butterflies may not live long, but at least they spend the time they have free in the sunshine."

Lorne tried to break in, but Raymond kept speaking. "We've destroyed their habitat, the flowers, the trees. Even the milkweed my monarchs need is mostly gone. But there is still air. They fly free. And the sunshine is still clean. The sun is still — "

The camera switched abruptly to the host. "That's all the time we have right now, folks. When we return from these messages from our sponsors, we bring you a profile of one of the gladiators you'll see later tonight." The scene switched to a burly man dressed only in a piece of cloth twisted about his loins. His skin was beaded in sweat and he scowled at something behind the camera.

"I fought him this afternoon." Abigail sounded bored but her shoulders were rigid. "Big, but slow. Took me only five minutes to kill him."

Perry's mind was still on Raymond's segment. "They'll never air that."

"Yes, they will," Abigail said. "They've got plans for your friend."

"What do you mean?" Perry asked, but then the green room door crashed open and Raymond stumbled in, almost as if he'd been pushed. He clutched his hat to his chest, and his hands trembled.

"He wasn't interested in my butterflies at all." He turned an angry face to Perry. "He just wanted to talk about killing them."

Perry didn't know what to say. He thought about pointing out that this was Death TV, after all, but that seemed kind of obvious.

Raymond blinked, his eyes moist. "Why doesn't anyone want to talk about life?"

"I do." Abigail sat beside him. "There's been too much death in my life. And you know what?" She took his hand in hers. "I've never seen a butterfly."

Raymond spoke, his grip on his hat gradually loosening. He spoke of skippers and swallowtails, admirals, and hairstreaks. He talked about butterflies that used to be found in alpine meadows and marshes and woodlands. "In courtship often the female flutters on a flower or plant, while the male hovers over her before they mate. But in other species, the two fly straight up, in a sort of complex dance." His face was alight now, eyes glowing, and he clasped his hands together at his heart, his hat tumbling unnoticed to the floor. "Oh, that must have been wonderful to see."

He had begun to speak about the protective colouration of larvae and adult butterflies when the door opened and Tina came in. "You're on," she said to Abigail. Then she gestured at Raymond. "Him, too."

"What?" Perry and Raymond turned to stare at her. Abigail simply nodded. "I told you," she said to Perry.

Tina grabbed Raymond's shoulder, hauled him to his feet, and turned to face the mirrored wall. Perry, with a cold grab in his heart, knew the camera was on.

"Raymond Baines," she said to the camera, "a condemned criminal, has been brought to justice and you are viewing this drama live on Death TV."

"Condemned?" Perry snapped around.

A man, wearing the purple cloak of a court official, stepped into the green room.

"Read the charges," Tina intoned.

The man cleared his throat. "This man — "

"No," Tina hissed. "Face the camera."

The man glanced shyly at the mirror, slicked a hand across his hair, and started again. "This man, Raymond Baines, stands convicted of the following charges. Fifteen years ago, in August of 2012, he participated in an environmental demonstration in DC. A bomb was detonated and three public servants and one police officer died. Those directly involved in this violence were condemned to death. Those who, like Baines, were present but could prove they had no foreknowledge of the bomb, were sentenced to ten years in prison."

Perry grabbed the man's arm. "If Raymond wasn't sentenced to death, then he can't be taken to the arena."

The official shook him off. "I'm not finished. Move away or I'll have you arrested for obstructing justice." He smiled at the camera, puffed out his chest, and continued. "During the power shortages of the late teens, it became necessary to ration power to certain civilian sectors. One area affected was the prison system.

"It soon became apparent this was a mistake, for the prisoners, without power to run their TVs, became restive and in some cases, violent. One such uprising took place at the penitentiary where Baines was incarcerated. He and several others took advantage of the confusion to escape. Most were recaptured but Baines apparently moved here to Philadelphia and avoided judiciary notice. That situation has now come to an end."

He turned, making sure his profile was still available to the camera, and addressed Raymond. "Raymond Baines, prison escape is a capital offense. The citizens of the United States demand justice, and you are hereby sentenced to death."

Perry stood in stunned silence. In Tina's grasp, Raymond began to struggle.

Tina grinned at Abigail, her grip on Raymond holding firm. "You know that gladiator who was causing all the trouble before? Bastard tried to run away and a guard had to kill him. Didn't happen in front of a camera, either. So we're short a gladiator, and we're already behind schedule." She turned to Raymond. "You're lucky. Your sentence can be carried out right away."

"He can't fight," Abigail said. "Look at him. He won't last thirty seconds."

"Take me instead." Perry, to his surprise, found himself on his feet and heard these words coming out of his mouth. He held up his arm, flexed his biceps. "I'm pretty good in a fight."

Tina looked shocked. "We can't put an innocent man in the arena. And besides, the top brass liked your Siren Call cube. A lot. They'd want you to stick around to shoot more for the show." She began to haul Raymond out of the room.

His face was blank, his body limp. Then he stood up straight, dug his heels in, and pulled his shoulder free from Tina's grip. He bent and picked up his hat and turned to Perry and Abigail. "I knew it was a risk to come on TV, but I thought of the good I could do, telling people about butterflies. You listened, and I thank you. I have some at home, monarchs, ready to come out of their cocoons. They might be out now, drying their wings, ready to take to the air. But they'll be trapped in the glass jars." His face crumpled suddenly. "This can't be happening." He turned wildly to Tina, but she stood, arms crossed, blocking the door.

Perry also couldn't believe this was happening. "This isn't right."

Tina shrugged. "One of his co-workers turned him in. That man will receive a special Death TV reward."

"But," Perry said, "you shoot deaths that are happening anyway. You don't create death."

Tina smiled. "The capture of escaped criminals is of great interest to our viewers. Raymond's co-worker deserves his reward."

Perry stared at her, wondering who she was beneath the bright veneer. He wondered, too, who he was himself. "Goodbye, Raymond," he said softly.

Raymond stared at him, then at Abigail. "Goodbye, Raymond? I guess it is." He reached out and took Perry's hand. "I want you to call me Ray. It's what my mother used to call me. I was her little ray of sunshine, she said." His eyes shone with tears. "She was in the tunnel under the river when it collapsed. Alone in the dark. No ray of sunshine with her when she died."

"Come on. We're running late." Tina grabbed Ray's arm and pulled him from the room. Abigail, with one last unreadable look at Perry, followed.

Perry sank down on a couch and buried his face in his hands. Death came to everyone. Why should it be different if it came from a speeding train or a stray bullet, or from being drafted to fight in the arena?

He didn't know the answer. But somehow it mattered, mattered so much he didn't even think about what Tina had said about how the top brass had liked his cube so much they wanted more from him. He didn't think about how his dream was coming true. He thought only of Ray's dream of butterflies, flying free in the sunshine.

ꧻꧻꧻ

On the TV screen, the woman held her dying child tightly against her breast as a bullet slammed into her neck. A man rushed into the camera frame, glanced wildly about. For one moment his eyes, grey and cold, looked directly into the lens, directly into the eyes of the viewers, then he raised his pistol to his temple and pulled the trigger. The camera panned over the three fallen bodies, caressed them with slow movement across twisted limbs and empty faces. In the background, sirens wailed as the scene faded to black.

Throughout the bar, cheers erupted. Hands slapped Perry on the back, punched him on his arms. Peter plucked him from his bar stool and enfolded him in a bear hug.

"And now," said a voice from the TV, "we meet the young man who stood behind the camera during this touching drama. Let's give a warm welcome to Perry Hendrin."

Applause and cheering burst from the TV. Perry, breathless from Peter's hug, sat back down and watched himself walk through a studio audience on his way to the raised dais at the front of the room. He hadn't realized until he was told to enter the studio that the segment was being shot in front of a live audience and he'd stood, stunned for a long moment before he took his first step and the waves of applause broke against him.

"Congratulations," the host said to Perry on the TV. "That was one fine piece of camera work. Tell us how it came about."

On the TV, Perry talked about his radio and his motorcycle, how he listened for calls to police and ambulance, and had heard the code meaning a domestic dispute. In the bar, Perry watched the TV and felt distant from the young man on the screen. He saw again the face of the mother as she picked up her dying baby, his head split from the father hurling him against a wall, the mother's surprise and then acceptance as she fell to the ground in front of her house. She'd ignored his camera lens, had looked only at her child, but the father had faced the camera and grinned as he raised the gun to his head. He'd grinned, and Perry had grinned, too, filled with the exultation of knowing what he'd just recorded was good enough to get on *Siren Call.* He'd been on one side of the camera and the dead people were on the other side. Their deaths would last forever, because of him.

But now the Perry on TV seemed very small, a puppet jerking through responses pulled out of him by the host's questions. Perry looked down at the bar and took a big gulp of beer. He'd drunk four already, and hadn't had to pay for a single one. He was the big hero tonight.

The show ended and Perry watched himself, smiling at the camera as it panned from him to the ecstatic audience. The scene faded out and the familiar Death TV logo filled the screen.

"Stay tuned," said a voice-over. "When we return, we bring you a very special moment in television history — the first show in what is destined to be our most popular program ever — *Arena.*"

Mike sat on the other side of Peter. "Do you think," he asked, "that if I commit a murder I'll have a chance to get on *Arena*?"

The screen suddenly lit up in a blaze of light. Only vague shadows could be seen, arms lifting weapons, bodies braced against blows. The sounds were vivid, clash of sword against shield, grunts, harsh breathing. Then the light shifted and an image of a woman gladiator filled the screen. Abigail.

Perry pushed himself off his stool, bumping Peter as he stood up. Peter ignored him, his eyes glued to the screen. Perry stumbled backwards, holding a hand up between his face and the TV. He didn't want to see Raymond die. He didn't want to see anyone die. He turned and ran from the bar.

On his bike, the night dark around him, he filled the empty streets with the roar of his engine, downshifting, screaming around corners, pushing the revs to the limit. He ignored the Airomatic and goggles, welcoming the pain in his lungs and eyes. He skidded on gravel, knew the bike could go down, held it by sheer strength and force of will. He screamed towards a crumbling brick wall, slammed on the brakes, wasn't sure if he'd stop in time, and didn't care.

Is there a difference? he wondered. Between shooting death as it happens and arranging for it to happen so you can shoot it? The people want to watch death, death that's everywhere, and yet is far removed when it happens on a screen.

He criss-crossed the city, passing crumbling buildings and walled mansions, bars filled with laughing people and sidewalks where people slept, fought, made love. He rode until the light of false dawn began to gray the eastern sky.

He thought of Ray and wondered why it mattered so much that this man was dead. He hoped Abigail got her twenty-five kills so she could live on, but wished it hadn't been Raymond who helped her stay alive. His cheeks felt funny, stiff and hot, and he brushed a hand across his eyes. His fingers came away wet.

It was the butterflies, he thought. The damn butterflies. They were out of their cocoons and had no way out of their jars. Ray had been so looking forward to going home and seeing them.

Perry screeched to a halt at a callbooth. The unit's casing was half-pulled from its mount, and someone had scratched initials and a heart on the screen, but Perry keyed in "Raymond Baines" and a number and address were displayed.

Perry had no key, but Ray's lock was a cheap one and this wasn't the first time Perry had entered where he hadn't been invited. He stepped into Ray's room and flipped on the light.

Ranged on the mantelpiece, reflecting silver in the light, was a row of jars. In each one, wings flapping against the glass walls, was an orange and black butterfly. A lump swelled in his throat until he could hardly breathe.

He opened a jar. The butterfly took a few moments to discover the opening, then it flew up and out. It flew directly towards the light. Perry, horrified, rushed to turn it off, afraid the butterfly would burn itself.

With the light off, the room was very dark, even though the sun was rising outside. Ray's window faced the next-door building's blank wall, so there was no way for the low sun to find its way in. Perry stood in the dark, unmoving, and listened. Something brushed his cheek, soft, there and then gone. He edged along the wall until he reached the window, opened it and stood waiting.

Nothing happened. Then he heard a sound. Not the soft flutter of a butterfly, this was loud and hard. Someone was on the other side of the door.

Perry backed up until he bumped against the mantel. The door opened, the light was flipped on. There, framed in the doorway, stood Ray.

Perry's eyes widened. He ran across the room and hugged Ray. "You're alive. But how — ?"

Ray didn't seem to care that Perry had broken in to his apartment. His eyes went to the row of glass jars. "They've emerged," he said, and went to them, his fingers caressing the glass wherever a butterfly brushed it.

Perry glanced about the room. The butterfly he'd freed was gone. It must have found the window. He pictured it, outside but trapped between two walls with no way to go but up. Up, towards the sky.

"We have to take them outside." Ray began picking up jars, cradling them against his chest. His top hat was gone, and his white shirt was splashed with blood. "Usually I send them to one of the greenhouses outside of the city, but there's not time."

"Ray." Perry picked up a jar, too. "I'm glad you're here, and I don't want to sound as if I doubted you, but how did you survive the arena?"

Ray looked at him, eyes suddenly blank. "It was Abigail. She killed herself. Put her hand on mine on the hilt of my sword and pulled it into . . . " A tear rolled from his eye and splashed on a jar lid. "She fell. She reached up and pulled me down beside her. She said, she said . . . " He ducked his head and tried to wipe his eyes but his arms were full of jars. The butterflies, agitated by the movement of their prisons, flapped wildly.

"She said," Ray continued, looking Perry full in the face, "that she was already dead. Twenty-five was too large a number. Anyone who killed that many times was the walking dead. But me, I was alive. She wanted me to stay that way. And," he looked down at the jars he held, "she asked me to describe butterflies to her while she died." He took in a deep heaving breath. "I only had time to tell her about the brilliant yellow on an orange barred sulphur, and I was just getting into eyespots and other protective markings, when . . . when she . . . "

He stood very still and wept, hugging his jars. Perry quietly picked up the rest.

"I left, then," Ray said. "As a winner I was supposed to fight again, but I just walked out. They'll be coming for me."

Perry remembered what Abigail had said — "big plans for your friend." If Ray had left the Death TV building it was because he'd been allowed to leave. It seemed the network's plans for him weren't over yet.

Ray closed his eyes for a moment. "I'll just think about the butterflies." He looked at the jars, and noticed his bloody shirt. "I should change." He headed over towards the hooks in the wall where his few clothes hung, but then stopped. "No. On second thought it seems right that part of Abigail is with us when the butterflies fly free." He walked to the door, still open from when he'd come in, and left. Perry followed, carrying the last of the jars.

Outside, the sun was balanced on the tops of buildings visible across a vacant lot. The air scorched his throat. Perry could see the taller buildings of downtown, their outlines blurred by smog. A glint of light stabbed his eyes, and he turned to see the sun reflecting off a camera lens held by someone hidden in a clump of bushes. The butterfly release was being filmed. Perry didn't know why, and he didn't care, not even if it meant he'd have another chance to be on TV.

Ray opened a jar, then another, and Perry followed suit. When all the jars were empty, the two men stood back and watched the small cloud of butterflies, black and orange, fly around each other, spiralling up into the open air.

Perry, glancing toward the bushes, saw that the glint from the camera had been joined by another, dark and malevolent. He reached for Ray, started his dive to the ground, and realized he wasn't the only person who spent time thinking up new programming ideas for Death TV. What would it be called? *Citizen's Arrest*? *Vigilante*? Whichever, someone, he thought with a tinge of envy as the gun went off, had come up with a sure-fire winner.

Gated

A SIREN WAILED. THE DOG howled. The boy, as always, was drawn to the window.

It was dark out, the only memory of the sun a sullen red glow that silhouetted the tops of buildings in the community across the street. A light shone in the upstairs window of a house directly across from his. Kevin wondered, as always, if another boy stood there, also gazing out at the flashing red and blue lights. Red and blue reflections on the outside wall meant a police car. He wondered where it was going.

Kevin headed downstairs. At the dining room table, his father shuffled through piles of tax forms. Three months had gone by quickly, Kevin thought, if it was tax time again.

Kevin's father ignored sirens. Everyone did, except the dog. It lived in the community across the street. Maybe it belonged to the other boy who maybe also went to the window when a siren wailed. No one in Kevin's community had a dog. That was one of the rules here.

"A new tax," his father said, "on all products that contain reinforced aluminum. A tax increase on baby food and children's clothing."

"Crime is increasing," Kevin's mother said from the kitchen. He heard the rattle of the ice in her glass as she poured another cup of EZ-Soothe. It was her fifth that evening. "The city needs more police. Crime affects us all and we should all be happy to pay for the brave men and women who protect us."

"You spend too much time in front of a screen." Kevin's father sorted through more forms. "Why do you repeat everything you hear? Learn to think for yourself."

"Like you?" Kevin's mother walked unsteadily through the kitchen door and collapsed onto a chair.

"Yes, like me. The gated communities have no crime. It's a problem of the inner city. Why should we pay for services we don't need?"

Kevin looked out the window, but the sound of the siren had faded and he couldn't see the road. The wall surrounding his community was too high. He sat down at the wallscreen set into an alcove beside the kitchen door. He finished the last of his Civics homework, a list of ten reasons his community made its people happy, and then clicked on his favourite game, Little Old Lady Bowling. The Community Message Board flashed on, as it always did when someone opened a new program, this time in big balloony letters coloured pink and blue: *Everyone is responsible for everyone else in a caring community like ours.*

The little old ladies were set up at the far end of the bowling alley. Before he could throw his first ball, the banner announcing breaking news flashed across the top of his screen. The game went blank.

Kidnapping! flowed across the screen in square red letters. "A twelve year-old girl, Margaret Pangton, was kidnapped from her inner city home, vanishing while she played in the broken rubble of a vacant lot. Her mother alerted the authorities but despite an intensive search, the small number of police available at the time was unable to find her. The next morning her body was found at the local landfill. The mayor and police chief announce their sorrow at the loss of this child from our community. When asked by your reporter on the spot, they admitted that, had there been more money budgeted for community security, a larger police force might have been able to find the girl in time. The mayor added. 'With things the way they are, well, we do our best.' This is Alan Gee, reporting for Community News."

The computer fell silent and Kevin stared at the expanse of oiled hardwood awaiting his bowling ball. The dead girl was the same age as his older sister. Why hadn't there been enough police to find her and save her? He turned to his father, his stomach churning. "It's good that we pay taxes," he said.

Kevin's father threw down his pen. "Just like your mother. Do you have to repeat everything on the community screens? Next you're going to be telling me that those of us lucky enough to live in a gated community show their love for the larger city community by paying taxes."

Why else would anyone pay taxes, Kevin wondered, but he could tell his father wasn't in the mood to answer questions. He returned to his game, but it had lost its appeal. He went upstairs and looked out his bedroom window.

What would it be like to live outside walls, not to see their secure presence no matter which direction he looked? The walls were almost as high as a second storey window, built of red brick veneer covering concrete. His house was near the front wall, beside the community garden. His was one of the larger gated communities, with over 5000 people. They had two doctors and a factory that made disposable diapers. They even had apartment blocks, although they, too, were only two stories high. Sometimes one of the doctors had to use the community armoured car to go to a smaller gated community that needed him. And once a portrait painter had come to Kevin's house, to paint Kevin and his sister. The painter had arrived in his community's armoured car.

Kevin liked to watch the armoured cars, the way the shields rose to cover the car's windows when it left the gate and went down when it returned. It was lucky the cars had the route programmed, so the people inside could be completely shielded from the dangers outside the walls. Kevin had never been outside. Most people hadn't.

Another siren let out a cry, the flashing lights red and white this time. Ambulance. The dog cried too, its voice rising from a low mutter to a high-pitched throbbing howl. The only time Kevin ever heard the dog make noise was when it heard a siren. He felt a kinship with the dog because sirens made it sad, too.

He'd tried talking to his school counselor about how sirens made him feel. "Sirens are good," she'd said. "They mean help is on the way."

"But they mean help is needed," Kevin wanted to add, but he didn't. Why did nobody else care about the people inside the ambulances, the people the police were rushing to protect, the people whose houses were burning up? All anybody cared about was that the sirens were outside the walls.

He thought about the kidnapped girl. There'd been no walls to protect her. The police had tried to save her, they really had.

That wasn't fair. If there weren't enough police and if people like his father grumbled when they had to pay more taxes so there could be more police, then something else had to be done. People who lived inside walls should be doing more to help. They could walk around and look for missing people like Margaret, find out where she liked to play. Kevin had a favourite spot, the park behind the third row of houses. Margaret might have been at her favourite spot, and if there'd been other kids around, maybe she'd have been safe.

ꕥꕥꕥ

Kevin couldn't stop thinking about the murdered girl and his sister. Moyra was mean sometimes, but he still didn't want her dead. Maybe Margaret Pangton had a brother who was sad she was dead.

The police were probably sad, too. The police he watched onscreen, on the show *Policeman Knows Best*, were never sad because they never failed to save people. But Kevin knew that real life wasn't always the same as the shows. His shoulders slumped as he realized the real life police were sad. He had to do something to help them. If there wasn't enough money for more police, then people like him would have to help them. He would have to go outside the walls to where he was needed.

He didn't know how to get outside. The big gate would be locked, or so he assumed, because nobody ever tried to open it. But one morning he heard that the doctor who worked with bones had been called to another gated community. Kevin hid in a bush beside the gate, and once the doctor was gone, and the people who liked to watch the armoured car had turned away, and the steel doors were swinging silently together and were almost shut, he slipped outside.

Behind him, the gate closed without a sound. In sudden panic, he spun to look at it. A wave of nausea swept through him. He sank to the ground and shut his eyes tight. Slowly the dizziness ebbed, and he opened one eye and then the other. He looked across the road. The wall and gate of the community across the street stood there, tall and strong.

Kevin had seen vids at school, of course, from the times when crops like wheat and corn were grown outside in huge fields instead of in hydropon glasshouses. They were just pictures, though. Now, for the first time, he was outside. He slowly stood up and faced the road. A view ran into the distance with no wall to block his sight.

The road went in both directions for a very long way. On either side of it were walls. Each wall protected a gated community. Attached to the wall next to each gate was a metal shape. All the ones Kevin could see were birds. He recognized a swallow and a hawk. His community had an eagle. That made sense. When Kevin's mother ordered groceries that weren't in the community store, she typed in the word *eagle* when asked where to deliver it.

As his heartbeat slowed and his head cleared, other details came into focus. The road was smooth and black, different from the brick walkways in his community. There were no trees, nothing green at all. Poles ran along each side of the road, much taller than him but not as high as the walls, thick and round, evenly spaced. Some had speakers bolted to the top, others held banks of lights. He started walking in the direction he hoped would take him to the inner city.

After a while it got easier facing the open road and he was able to walk without trailing his hand along the comforting presence of the walls beside him. I'm really outside, he thought, and started to run.

"I'm outside. I'm alone," he yelled. He kicked one of the poles, tried to climb it to reach the lights it held, but the surface was too slippery.

He ran a long way. He'd never realized there were so many gated communities. He was tired. Back home his mother would be dialling up lunch, and the thought made his stomach rumble. But he had to keep going. The police needed his help.

Up ahead, the road snaked into a bend. Kevin glanced back, seeing only the road lined with walls. He wondered if he'd be able to recognize his own community when he went home, if it was too dark to see the eagle. The walls all looked the same. But the police would help him, he was sure. Maybe they'd even give him a ride in a police car or ambulance, with siren wailing and lights flashing.

He heard a siren now. It approached from around the bend, and he could see red lights reflecting on the curved wall. The siren grew rapidly louder, and he pressed himself against a wall and tried to be invisible. The wail grew closer, was almost on top of him, and he realized suddenly he shouldn't be trying to hide. He should be standing in the open, waving to the firemen, letting them know he was here to help. He pictured himself holding a hose, climbing a ladder, and knew they'd be so grateful they'd give him a fireman's hat of his very own.

He took a step out into the road just as the siren and lights were upon him, and suddenly they whipped past and were gone, receding into the distance. There were no firemen to wave to. There was no fire truck rushing to help. The siren and lights were on the poles, sweeping from one to the next, along the road.

Kevin stood alone between walls and watched and listened as the lights and siren faded into the distance. His mouth hung open and he closed it with a snap.

What was going on? Were all the sirens that made him and the howling dog so sad nothing but speakers on poles? Surely there were people who needed help. Was there no one to hear their calls?

His solitude crashed through him, like a vid he'd seen of an ocean wave howling down on a small boat, and he sank to his knees. No walls to protect him now, or rather, walls all around him but they only kept him out.

A low hiss vibrated into his leg bones and he looked up, then jumped to his feet. An armoured vehicle, larger than his community's car, rode smoothly around the curve and came to a stop beside him. A door opened and a man wearing a policeman's cap beckoned him inside.

"I knew it," Kevin said happily as he scrambled onto the back seat. "You do come to help." The windows were unshielded. This policeman must be very strong and brave.

The car rotated and headed back the way it had come. "It's nice of you to pick me up," Kevin said. "But how did you know I was coming?"

"Security cameras." The policeman gestured towards the poles and walls sliding past. "We keep watch."

Kevin nodded. "My mom was right. You don't have enough policemen to do the job. That's why I came outside."

The policeman said nothing more, and after a while the car drove past the last wall.

This must be the inner city. It must be because there were no more high walls. But this looked nothing like the images he saw most nights on the City Crime Reports. Onscreen, the houses looked like they were falling down, and many had windows that were broken or covered with wood. Here, the houses were beautiful, soaring or sprawling, all much bigger than anyone, even Doctor Richards, had at home. Lots of vehicles sat by each house, which meant these people could go outside the city if they wanted. These cars weren't even armoured, even though all the ones he'd seen on Community News were.

There were people on the street, women pushing babies in strollers, kids running, a couple of men standing on a walkway, their heads close as they talked. Some of the people waved at the car as it went by, and the policeman waved back.

The people looked healthy. Nothing like the inner city people shown onscreen, where people's skin was pale and they hunched their shoulders when they walked outside, and peered fearfully about. These people had no walls to protect them, and they looked happy.

The car came to a stop in front of a large grey building. Stairs led up to a double door, but this door wasn't a gate. It had glass panels and above the door were the words *Police Station*.

Kevin bounded up the stairs beside the policeman. The station looked just like the one on the show *Cop Pride*. "This is great. Are you going to assign me to a patrol? Will I have a partner?"

The policeman said nothing, just held a door open for Kevin to pass inside.

Facing the door was a high counter and more police stood behind it. The man with Kevin nodded and said, "Tell him he's here," and took Kevin to a small room lined with chairs. "Stay here," he said. "The chief wants to see you."

Kevin sat down, legs swinging. The chief! They must really need his help. No doubt the chief of police was going to assign Kevin to something very important. Maybe he'd get to interrogate a suspect!

He waited a long time. At first he wondered why, if they needed him so badly, they were making him wait. Then he decided that no doubt the chief was very busy with other important things, and was just as unhappy as Kevin that they couldn't have their meeting right away.

A few other people sat in the room with him, men and women. No one spoke. A woman beside Kevin rubbed her shoe on the floor, up and down, making little scraping noises. Once in a while a policeman would bring someone new or call a name and take somebody away.

Kevin had to go to the bathroom. He sat as still as he could, but couldn't help wriggling as his bladder grew fuller. He quietly slid off his chair. No one paid any attention, so he moved to the door. Looking up and down the hallway he spied the familiar sign showing a stick man.

After rushing down the hall and using the men's room, he felt better, and braver, too. No one would be angry that he'd left the waiting room. He was needed. He was important. He walked a little further down the hall, away from the waiting room, and came to another room with chairs. This one had deep comfortable chairs, not the little wooden chairs in the waiting room. It had a coffee machine, and a wallscreen showing *The Car and Truck Hour,* one of Kevin's favourite programs. No one was in the room so he stepped just inside the doorway.

The screen was showing a vehicle as big as an armoured car, but without the steel plates, when the breaking news banner moved across the top. The big red letters that read, *Kidnapped!* appeared, and the girl's face shown was the same as the one he'd seen on his screen at home. Kevin didn't think he wanted to hear the same story again, as it had made him so sad, but he did want to see if the truck's windows really went up and down, so he stayed.

"A twelve-year-old girl, Margaret Pangton," the screen read, "was kidnapped from her gated community, vanishing while she played in the schoolyard. Her mother alerted the authorities but despite an intensive search, the small number of police available at the time was unable to find her. The next morning her body was found stuffed into one of the gated community's dumpsters. The mayor and police chief announce their sorrow at the loss of this child from our community. When asked by your reporter on the spot, they admitted that, 'had there been more money budgeted for community security, a larger police force might have been able to find the girl in time. With things the way they are, well, we do our best. We are fortunate that our undesirables are shut away behind the walls of the gateds, but we still need our police to keep all people safe.' This is Alan Gee, reporting for Community News."

Kevin's knees went wobbly and he took a step back, only keeping himself from falling by grabbing the door frame. A heavy hand fell on his shoulder.

"I thought I told you," the hand squeezed him hard, "to stay where I left you." It was the policeman who'd driven him here, and he sounded angry. "The chief is ready for you."

Kevin looked up at the man and nodded. His mind swirled with a blizzard of thoughts. The same girl couldn't have been killed both in the inner city and in a gated community. Why did the reporter say that undesirables lived in gated communities? He was too busy thinking to wonder much about the important job the chief was going to give him.

The man kept a heavy hand on his shoulder as they walked upstairs. They went into a room with a window looking out over the happy people and beautiful houses that didn't exist according to all the news items Kevin had ever seen about the inner city, and then into an office. It was big enough for a couch and two puffy chairs arranged around a low table, as well as a desk, but Kevin paid only enough attention to keep from bumping into things. The policeman led him to stand in front of the desk, then left. Kevin stared at the floor, but eventually the fact that he was here with the chief broke through the thoughts that darted and scraped through his mind, and he looked up.

The chief sat in a large black chair, the kind that could spin round and round. His hands were folded, resting on his rounded stomach, and his round face was split into a smile. "So you came to help," he said.

Kevin nodded.

The chief leaned forward and placed both hands flat on his desk. "Well, that's wonderful. You'll be a very big help, indeed."

"I will?" Kevin's voice sounded very small in his ears. "Why are the sirens only speakers on poles?"

"They're there to let the crooks know we're coming, of course."

That made sense, kind of. Kevin tried to think about crooks committing crimes along the lonely road, witnessed only by the blank walls of the gated communities. What was there to do there that was so terrible? Before he could ask about this, the chief stood up and came around his desk. He pulled off his cap. "Would you like to wear this?"

Would he? Questions about crimes, and cameras and lights on poles, vanished. The chief set the cap on Kevin's head, and it settled over his brow. He pushed it up from his eyes and grinned.

"Come," the chief said. "There's no time to waste. We have a very important job for you."

"What will I be doing?" Kevin asked, but the chief was already walking out the door so Kevin had to run after him.

They went down a flight of steps, wide steps made of shiny wood with a darker wood banister, along a hall, and down another staircase, this one with steps of grey cement. The chief pulled open a heavy steel door and led Kevin into the dark space beyond. A man was sitting behind a glass wall, staring at a whole row of screens. Most of them showed streets in the inner city, and a couple seemed to be views of gated communities. Two showed the road between the walls.

The man came out to where Kevin and the chief were. "Another one?" he asked.

Kevin looked around. He stood on a grey platform that overlooked a larger space. No lights were on, only glints here and there, small against the larger dark.

"Sorry to work you so hard, Mac," the chief said. "Make sure this one is found close to, but outside, his community. Eagle."

Kevin walked tall, so the too-big cap stayed balanced on his head. This new man wasn't wearing a police uniform, and he was very tall with heavily muscled arms. Kevin didn't like the way the man looked at him, as if Kevin was a thing, not a person wearing the chief's hat. But then the man smiled at him, just for a moment, and Kevin realized they were talking about taking him home.

"Gated, huh," Mac said.

The chief stuck his finger in Mac's chest. "Different spin this time. We want to make sure they know that coming outside is not only dangerous, it's deadly."

Mac shrugged. "Whatever you say. But it'll seem funny, another kid."

"Maybe having a real kid this time will be good. We can say he came out to prey on innocent city folk."

"I came to help," Kevin said hotly. He decided he didn't like these people very much, but they were the police, so they had to be good.

Mac stepped back into his booth and flipped a switch. A single light came on in the darkness, and it shone down on a shiny ambulance. It was just as Kevin had imagined, white with big green crosses painted on the sides.

"You get to ride in the back, kid," the chief said. Mac returned and opened the double doors at the back of the ambulance.

"My name's Kevin." He peered inside. There didn't seem to be anything in there, not even a bed for a sick person, but it was dark and hard to see.

"Don't be afraid, Kevin," the chief said. "You don't need to be." The chief grabbed his cap off of Kevin's head. "Fear is only for those who pay taxes."

Kevin turned to stare at the chief, but Mac picked him up and tossed him into the ambulance. Before he could even scramble to his knees, the doors clanged shut.

Inside, it was very dark. The vehicle eased into smooth motion. Fear fluttered, beating Kevin with the wings of black birds. He tried the doors. Locked. He pounded on the front, behind where he figured Mac was sitting. No response.

The ambulance picked up speed, and then the siren came on. Kevin sat in the dark, surrounded by walls. I am a wall, he thought, and all that's inside me is a distant wail. The siren was very loud and, as always, spoke to him of nothing but sorrow.

ꙮꙮꙮ

A siren wailed. The dog howled. The boy, as always, was drawn to the window.

A light shone in the upstairs window of a house in the community directly across from his, and Thomas wondered if another boy stood there, also gazing out at the reflections of flashing red and white lights. Red and white meant ambulance. He wondered where it was going.

The dog howled again, a quavering rise in pitch that hung in the growing darkness. The dog belonged to a neighbour. Thomas used to worry about it when it howled. He wondered if someone was hurting it and that was why it cried. He went to see it sometimes, but it always looked healthy enough. He decided that it, like him, was made sad by sirens.

Lifting Weights

"THERE'S NO REASON FOR Superman to have big muscles."

"Huh?" Jane looked across the gym dome at her friend.

"Think about it," Sandra continued. "Muscles get larger when they encounter resistance. If he's so strong on Earth because of his dense molecular structure and because there's a yellow rather than a red sun, then he encounters no resistance. Everything is easy for him. No resistance, no reason to grow big muscles."

It did make sense. Jane bent at the knees to pick up an eighteen kilogram barbell. On Earth she did biceps curls with a thirteen, but here on Sevrin 2, .75 gravity meant she could lift more. It still felt the same, though, an effort after the first five or so reps, and it still had the same non-visible effect. Here at least she knew the exercise was keeping her from losing muscle mass and bone density, but like on Earth, no amount of exercise had any effect on her thin body. She was a nerd and a wimp, a nerd who lifted weights, but a wimp all the same.

"I always liked Batman best," she said. "He was a real person, with only the abilities any of us might have."

"And he knew he could get hurt," Sandra said. "Superman only feared kryptonite."

"Superman could have been a little skinny fellow." Jane moved on to leg presses, ninety kilograms, a weight she could never have done at home. "And he would have been just as strong."

"Yes." Sandra had a barbell across her shoulders and was doing squats. Her face glistened with a sheen of sweat but she was still beautiful. Jane wondered how she could be friends with someone who made her feel inadequate in so many ways.

"But he wouldn't look heroic then," Sandra continued. "Can you see a comic book with a short skinny balding guy on the cover?" She moved into a weightlifting pose, one arm flexed over her head, one leg bent at the knee. "Superman. Faster than a speeding bullet, invulnerable, and he looks like the school kid everyone picked on."

Jane had been the school kid everyone picked on. "People wouldn't buy that comic."

Sandra grinned. "Right. So the hero has to look the part, tall, handsome, muscular. But you and I know his secret. Since he's never encountered resistance, there's no way he could have grown those bulging biceps. He pumps air into surgically-implanted muscle-shaped sacs."

Jane laughed. "He wears lifts."

"And a toupée."

"It's sad, though." Jane pushed damp brown hair out of her eyes. "Why couldn't we value a hero because of what he does, rather than how he looks?"

"Image, hon." Sandra slung a towel around her neck. "Everything's image these days."

Jane nodded. Her friend was right, as always, but she was glad image hadn't been all that mattered for getting a position here. Although, had it? A doctorate in xenopsychology, experience working on digs on Earth, papers published in the right journals, were those things her, or were they part of her image? She wasn't sure.

"I've got abs and stretches left," she said. "Are you done?"

"Yeah." The word was muffled as Sandra bent over her straight legs and put her head between her knees. "What do you have on for this afternoon?"

"Sherdville. I'll work on one of my jigsaws. What about you?"

"I think I might go back up the tel." Sandra glanced through the dome window. Jane, following her gaze, could see the hill, its even sides and flat top speaking of the buried treasure it contained. It was no longer as even or flat as it had been. Excavation had been going on for two years.

"There's a room," Sandra mused, "in that building by the well. It could be a storeroom, but I don't think so. It's off a tiny hallway, for one thing."

"I can take a look if you want," Jane offered.

"Sure. Maybe after supper."

Jane lay flat, put her hands behind her head, and began crunching.

ຮຮຮ

Jane wondered why she bothered to shower after a workout. Already, after having walked just a few hundred yards, sweat trickled under her arms. This reminded her of the dig in Israel, forty-eight degrees Celsius in the shade, blowing black mucous out of her nose after a shift because of the dust. At least here she didn't have to check her boots for scorpions before she put them on.

She glanced at the tel, wondering if Sandra was already up there. As sometimes happened, she was swept with a wave of wonder when she saw the jagged lines of walls and buildings silhouetted against the bleached sky. Intelligent beings had lived here for over seven thousand years.

The top layer at this dig was older by several hundred years than those at the other sites on this continent. The people here had all died, or they had left to join other communities, but why had they gone? They lived by a saltwater sea — fish bones had been found in sifted dirt — they must have had boats and known how to use them.

"There's everything higher life forms need, and it was here where this society vanished," Paul Detlam, the project head, had told her when she first arrived. "Grassland for grazing. Good soil for growing crops. The plant life was, and is, healthy."

Why, Jane wondered, is this peninsula populated only by birds and insects? Climate change? Paleobotanists had put the sifted dirt in flotation tanks, and found grains and chaff. The people hadn't starved. Attack by another race? Disease? Luckily, figuring out why the civilization was gone wasn't her job. Putting herself in the heads of the people who'd created it, was.

"C14 ratios put the top level at about eight hundred years old," Paul had said. "The lower levels, when we reach them, may tell us more."

A tarp provided some shade over Sherdville. The rows of tables were covered with bits and pieces of broken pottery, small metal objects, and the occasional bone or stone bead. Each was grouped according to where and when it had been found. Jane went to her table, where a partially completed figure, over a metre tall, taunted her with its inscrutable expression. She'd glued together the pieces she had and fashioned others to fit the smaller gaps, using FasDry. There were still large portions of the figure missing, and someone had left a bucket of pieces for her, hoping that perhaps one or two out of the several dozen there might belong to her current project.

Gaps or not, she had enough of the figurine to tantalize her. It was a woman, lush and voluptuous, with large eyes and a small pursed mouth. She had two arms and two legs, but hands sprouted all over her body: from her breasts, palms out, fingers splayed; from her groin, fisted; from her stomach, two hands with fingers interlaced.

The architecture uncovered so far suggested that the beings here had been humanoid, and this figure seemed to confirm that. But there had been very little representational art found. Household items, plenty of pots and bowls and clay bottles, were scattered on the tables, but only two other items showed people, and they were scratched drawings, showing the figures from a distance, one carrying a heavy bucket, the other kneeling over a prone smaller figure. None of these figures had extra hands, but the drawings were not in good condition, and smaller details could have been lost to time.

Jane studied the figurine, her head cocked to one side. Did the beings here have extra hands? Was this a representation of a deity? Was it an imaginary creature, perhaps used as a puppet might be, when telling stories? She looked again at the hands sprouting from the figure's breasts. They looked a little like hands held up in warning, a "don't come near" message. Could there have been women in this society who remained virgin? In that case, the fisted hand at the groin made sense, but what about the ones at the stomach? She sighed, picked up the most likely looking of the new fragments, and started fitting it to the gaps in the figure.

By the end of the day, as the sun sank towards the hills at the horizon, her back ached and her eyes were gritty and sore. She'd found two more small pieces of the figure, not a bad accomplishment for an afternoon's work. And some of the other sherds looked as if they belonged together, a water bowl, perhaps.

She headed for the communal kitchen dome, eager to see Sandra and find out what she'd learned about the mysterious room. She didn't catch sight of her friend among the micromorphologists and geologists and other scientists clustering about the serving table.

"Have you seen Sandra?" she asked them.

People did miss meals sometimes. Jane chewed absently on a piece of pita bread and went outside, gazing up at the tel. The setting sun was behind her, and details of the broken walls and dark openings into newly uncovered buildings glowed with a reddish reflection. Was Sandra still up there?

Surely, if she'd come down, filled with excitement and new discoveries about her room, she'd have found Jane to tell her about it. But maybe she wasn't alone. Maybe she'd met one of her current lovers up there, and they wouldn't appreciate being interrupted. She checked Sandra's tent. Empty. She could hardly check all of the men's tents, and sometimes narrowing down which of the men was one of Sandra's smitten swains, as the two women jokingly called them, was difficult.

She'd have to go up the tel. If Sandra was in trouble, there'd be no one there to help. Sandra was probably fine, just involved in a romantic encounter. She wouldn't bother anyone else with this, not unless she knew Sandra was in trouble. The team got up early and spent the morning excavating, before the sun grew too hot. During the fierceness of midday, they slept or spent time in the air-conditioned domes. Afternoons were spent in Sherdville or on other projects, and during the cooler evenings people either continued that work or went to sleep early.

Even though the sun was almost down, the air wasn't cool yet. Jane pushed her hair from her face and trudged up the side of the tel. This was the winter season here, with short days and long nights. This planet was closer to its sun, and had a shorter orbit, than Earth. There seemed to be only two seasons here near the equator, hot and hotter, and each lasted about five Earth months.

What did this blistering weather say about the people who not only survived, but flourished here? Jane reached the edge of the excavation level and surveyed what had been uncovered. The top of the tel looked vaguely like a waffle, roofless rooms dug out painstakingly, one bucket of carefully sifted dirt at a time. Her boots disturbed pebbles and dust, and she watched a group of stones clatter down a slope. How many of those stones had been here, undisturbed, for hundreds of years before being scattered by her careless step? And beneath her feet were more stones, more buildings and broken pots and figurines and who knew what other wonders. Layer upon layer, city built upon city, each civilization building on the ruins of the last one. What had these ancient peoples thought when they had to accept the evidence that life and society were not eternal? What drove them to try again when they knew others had failed?

The well was the lowest point on this level, and it extended down through all layers and into the ground below the bottom one. Someday one of the excavators would be lowered down there, but Paul wanted to wait until he knew more about the older layers. There were a few streams on the peninsula, one running from the mainland hills towards the tel before disappearing underground, a couple of others leaving the tel plain to make their way to the sea. Perhaps the well was sacred in some way. It must have been, as drawing water must have become increasingly difficult, since each city had to haul it up a greater distance.

Jane shrugged. So many questions. But right now the most urgent one concerned Sandra.

She knew the building that contained her friend's room. It was one of the few that still had a roof. She shone her wristlight along the hallway, so narrow her shoulders brushed either side. The room's entrance was an opening even tinier than the main doorway. She agreed with Sandra, there was no way this could be a storeroom, unless it had held only small objects. She placed a hand on either side of the opening, and peered in, looking for her friend. "Sandra?" Wide cracks ran across the hardpack floor. In one corner was a dark shadow her light couldn't penetrate. She took a step forward.

For a moment, it seemed the floor shook and the walls wavered, but she knew that was impossible. Then one of the cracks raced towards her, its edges jagged and hungry. She stood, eyes wide, forced her body to react, and took a step back, but suddenly there was no floor to step back onto.

She was instantly a child again, an eight-year-old who wanted to play with the other kids and who looked longingly out her bedroom window at the toboggan hill and the other kids laughing and screaming as they spun and soared down the hill. Jane wanted to slide, too, but her parents told her it was more important to practice her viola or study for school. She knew they told her she couldn't go because they were afraid the same thing would happen as the last time she tried to play with the kids, and that maybe this time she'd need more than just a couple of stitches. The people here didn't like the man who flew to the stars, who thought he was better than them since he could look down on them. While Jane had never heard her father say anything about looking down on anyone — mostly he looked away from Earth, wanting to travel further and further — the kids seemed so convinced of this that they hated her, too. Her parents refused to buy her a sled out of love, and they wanted her to do well in school so she, too, could someday fly to the stars. But she did well in school even without trying, and sledding looked fun.

Her father had bought her a new vidscreen, one of the new cubic ones, just before he went away again. The box it came in had been stored in the basement. She'd seen some of the kids sliding on plasboard, and it still looked like fun.

She lugged the box to the toboggan hill, knowing she should cut one side of it away to slide on, but not wanting to do that at home in case her mother looked up from her music. She was practicing with other people through a VirtLink, and didn't like to be disturbed, but you never knew, she might want a drink of water or something and wonder why Jane was cutting up a perfectly good box.

Jane arrived at the top of the hill breathless but triumphant, and tugged at one of the box flaps to tear it away. It was tough, harder than she'd expected, and while she pulled and tried different angles, a group of kids gathered around to watch and point and jeer.

"Look at Musclegirl," one boy crowed. "Thinks she's so superior and she can't even open a box."

"I bet she couldn't find her way out of a plastic bag," a girl screamed, jumping up and down.

"Can she find her way out of a box?"

"Let's find out!"

And before Jane had time to react, she was picked up and stuffed into the box and its flaps were sealed over her head, closing her off from the snow and the sky and the view of her home far below. The box scraped across the ground and then it pitched sharply down as it reached the edge of the hill. It rocked from side to side, moving faster and faster, hit a bump and flew into the air. Each time it landed, she was knocked from side to side, bouncing up and hitting down hard, until she no longer knew up from down.

When her world finally ceased to tumble, after one last hard blow that brought the box to a stop, she lay still, trying to breathe and not to cry. Her arm hurt a lot, more than anything ever had before. She heard the kids laughing, sliding again, and no one paid any attention to the crumpled box.

Even with her injured arm, she managed to unseal the box and crawl out. The box was tilted against a thick tree at the bottom of the hill, and she left it there, knowing she could get in trouble for littering the environment, but too hurt to carry it.

Her mother didn't say a thing about the box. After her broken arm was set Jane continued studying, and once the cast came off, playing viola, but the doctor never found the worst pain of all, the one inside, and so it never got set and it never healed. Her parents talked to the parents of the kids who'd put her in the box, and the kids apologized, but that just made them hate her more. And she never knew why they hated her so much, it couldn't just be because of her father's trips and because she got better marks in school — people judged other people according to who they were inside, right? That's what her father told her, and he was the smartest person she knew.

The hurt inside died down sometimes, but just as a badly set bone grew thick and ugly, it pushed at her from in her chest. As she grew older, sometimes there were people who liked her, and she treasured these few friends more than anything, more than her degrees, her awards, her publications, her promotions. But one thing that never lessened was her fear of being in dark enclosed spaces, and most of all, of falling in a dark enclosed space.

A wall fell towards her, a chunk of rock hit her wrist, smashing her light. The roof broke in two, in four, in countless parts, raining down on her. She covered her head, shutting her eyes to close out the dark, wondering if she'd be crushed, but how could she be, with no floor to be crushed against?

She fell through the darkness, her arm scraping the wall on one side, leaving behind what felt like at least a metre of skin, one foot finding the wall on the other side. She tried putting out her feet to either side, hoping to brake her fall, but then the passage narrowed, and she hit a ledge, bruising her tailbone. Then she was in a chute; suddenly it became a ridged slide, one that twisted back and forth, moving downward but with decreasing slope, so she was now sliding quite slowly. She coasted to a stop.

It was pitch dark. No, there was a light, a pinpoint some distance away. Was she still in the box? Was the light the other kids, coming to see how else they could torture her? But maybe, just maybe, there'd be one in whose eyes she'd see a little kindness, or at least regret for what they did to her.

The point of light was still there, waving about, although it hadn't yet illuminated her.

"Jane? Jane, is that you? What took you so long?"

"Sandra?" Jane pushed herself to her feet.

The light found her, dancing on her face for a moment before moving from her eyes. "I knew you'd come for me." Sandra's voice was as confident as always, and she put down the lantern and hugged Jane.

"How could you know?" Jane asked.

"Because you're my friend," Sandra said, as if explaining the simplest thing in the world, and Jane hugged her back.

"Are you hurt?" Sandra stepped away.

Jane shook her head and knuckled tears from her eyes. "No. Are you okay?"

"Yes." Her eyes glittered in the lantern light. "And let me show you what I've found." She darted off into the darkness.

Jane hastened after the light. Her scraped arm felt hot, and on investigating it with her other hand, she discovered it was bleeding. She thought about tearing a strip from her T-shirt to bind it and realized that, unlike in vids where the heroine's shirt tore neatly, just enough to reveal a tanned expanse of flat stomach, in her case the whole shirt would probably fall apart. She decided to ignore her arm.

Sandra hadn't gone very far. The lantern bathed her in a golden glow as she moved through a narrow tunnel. Then the light swooped up and out, becoming more diffuse, but reflecting off something ahead that sparkled in a way that was familiar.

Catching up, Jane saw a placid expanse of water stretching out before her.

"An underground lake. Did you suspect this?" she asked. "Is that why you came down here?"

Sandra laughed and shook her head. "No. I was poking around that little room, saw a crack in the floor, chipped at it with my pick, and the whole corner gave way beneath me."

"But what about the slide?" Jane stepped forward to the water's edge. From off in the distance, she heard a trickle. The lake must be stream fed.

"I think people from the lower levels used to come down here to worship the lake." Sandra pointed at a dark opening in the stone ceiling that stretched over the lake's cavern. "That's the bottom of the well. The slide may have originally been a pathway, or even stairs, worn smooth over the millennia."

Jane knelt and scooped up some water. It felt as water always did, wet and cool. She touched it to her lips. It tasted fine, but had an oily aftertaste which made her uneasy. The well water had been tested and found safe for human consumption, but no one drank it, preferring to use the distiller.

The smell made Jane realize she was thirsty. It was cooler here than on the surface, but the air was humid and still. "I don't suppose you brought some water?"

Sandra handed over a canteen. Drinking brought an image of the figure she'd been working on into Jane's head, and she wondered what the connection was. Hands? People used their hands to scoop water, or to build tools to get water. Then she had it. Drinking. The hands at the breasts could be a warning against a man's touch, but they could also hold off a baby. Maybe the figure was telling women not to breastfeed their babies.

But why? Surely there were no other ways to feed infants in a society as primitive as this one. Or had there been domestic animals? Cattle or goats to give milk?

"It's the only way." Sandra's voice snapped Jane out of her reverie.

"Breastfeeding?"

Sandra regarded Jane curiously. "Honey, I don't aim to be down here long enough where it's either starve or that. Besides, don't you have to have a baby first?"

Jane laughed, glad it was too dark for Sandra to see her blush. "What's the only way?"

"The well." Sandra pointed. "To get out."

Jane thought about the well, as seen from the top of the tel. She'd stayed away from it, and just the idea of approaching its crumbling stone wall and bending over to peer down made her dizzy.

"I tried going up the slide," Sandra continued. "Too slippery."

"We can't use the slide," Jane said slowly, "even if it wasn't slippery. The whole floor gave way when I fell. Your room is gone."

It was night. No one would be on the tel. And no one knew they were missing.

"Are you meeting a swain tonight?" she asked, hoping someone would notice they were gone.

"I told Michael maybe, if I wasn't too tired, but he probably gave up when I wasn't at supper."

There was no easy, or even possible, way out. The tel was over fifty feet high. It stood over her head, the walls and stones and pottery sherds and bones and who knew what else, all pulled down on her by gravity, less than on Earth, but that was still enough to crush her. And getting out meant going up, and going up meant time spent without solid ground under her feet. Black spots wavered before her eyes, and they didn't come from the lantern's uncertain light.

"Come here." Sandra didn't notice Jane's distress. "See where the well opens just above the water surface? I think if we swim out there, we can get inside and then find a way to climb up."

Jane looked. The cavern ceiling, high above where they stood, slanted lower over the centre of the lake, until it was just barely half a metre up. "Is there no other way?" she asked faintly.

"Nope," Sandra said cheerfully. "I looked around before you dropped in. There's the stream entering the lake at its other side, and so we could possibly swim out through there, but it runs underground and we have no way of knowing if there are air pockets."

Jane wondered if she'd rather face drowning than climbing and falling, but realized drowning was just another way of being enclosed in a dark place.

"Come on." Sandra at last noticed Jane's hesitation. "You can swim, can't you?"

Jane nodded. She could swim. She could at least swim out and look at the well from the bottom. There might be something of archaeological interest there, in the way it was constructed or the materials used, or . . .

"Are you okay?" Sandra asked. "Were you hurt when you came down?"

Jane wished she could say that was all it was. "I'm fine."

"You'll do good." Sandra rested a hand on Jane's shoulder. "We'll be together. I'll let you go up above me."

What? So I can knock you down, too, when I fall? But she let Sandra lead her into the water.

It was cold, but not unpleasantly so. It felt slightly thicker than lake water at home, but maybe that was just because every movement of her stiff body took so much effort. Her scraped arm hurt, but she followed Sandra, their splashes echoing in the cavern, until they arrived just beneath the well.

Sandra treaded water, peering up, and Jane moved in beside her. The lantern had been left on shore, and the well tunnel quickly became a black hole revealing no details. "Why can't we see the top?" Jane asked, hoping Sandra would assume the quaver in her voice came from being wet and cold.

"It's night." Sandra kicked with her legs and grabbed at the well. "That's too bad. If we could see daylight, we'd know the passage is straight."

"It has to be straight," the professional part of Jane said automatically. "If it wasn't, people couldn't get buckets up and down."

"You're so smart." Sandra grunted as she pulled herself up. The wall crumbled in her hands. "Can you support my weight so I can see what it's like in there?"

Jane ducked down so Sandra could kneel on her shoulders. The lake wasn't deep. She could keep her chin above water even bearing Sandra's weight. "Interesting." Sandra's voice drifted down. "Wood cribbing over stone."

Bits of sand and small stones rained down as Sandra did whatever it was she was doing. Jane felt numb, as if she was being swept along on a mighty river, with no control over where she went or what happened.

Sandra slipped off Jane, and came up beside her. "Back to back," she said. "A double layback."

"Back to back what?" Jane rubbed water from her eyes.

"Climbing. It's the only way. The sides are too smooth, and the well is too wide for the usual way of going up a chimney, a layback."

Jane didn't know. "What are you talking about?"

"Rock climbing. I've done it lots of times. When there's a shaft you need to get up, you wedge yourself in by pressing your feet against one wall and your back against the other."

Jane vaguely remembered seeing someone doing this in a vid. It had looked physically impossible and it didn't surprise her one bit that Sandra had done it. "But you said this well is too wide for that."

"Yup. That's why we do it back to back. We link arms behind us, and brace our feet on opposite sides."

"I suppose you've done this before?"

"No." Sandra grinned, her teeth white in the little light cast by the lantern. "Always a first time for anything. And with the lower gravity here, it just might be possible."

Jane looked longingly at the shore and the reassuring glow of the lantern. Maybe it would be better to stay there and wait for someone to find them. But how long would that take? There was no other way down here. And with the collapsed walls and roof, perhaps no one would know it was possible for anyone to fall in the small room. Oh, why hadn't she told someone where she was going?

Sandra climbed back on Jane's shoulders and reached into the well, clinging by her fingertips to a small ledge until she could swing her feet up. Spreading them as far as they could go, she was able to wedge each foot on opposite sides of the well, and reach down with a hand for Jane. Jane closed her eyes and tried to swallow, her throat dry, as she clambered into the darkness.

"You can support your weight on me." Sandra wasn't even breathing hard. "Put your feet against the wall and push your back against mine. Okay. Now think uplifting thoughts while I get this foot over to the other side."

All Jane could think of was the pile of nothing beneath her, soon to grow if this insane scheme of climbing actually worked. Her legs began to tremble. Sandra's back was warm against hers, but it was wet and slippery and she slid against it, feeling her bottom helplessly sagging down and then the rest of her folded in and she fell, landing with a splash in the lake.

Sandra splashed down beside her. "Okay," she said, laughing as if this was all some grand adventure. "We'll try that again. This time I'll move my leg around in smaller steps."

And so Jane found herself, knees bent, feet pressed flat against the well wall, her arms linked with Sandra's, their backs pressed snugly together.

"Isn't this cozy," Sandra said, and Jane could hear her smile in the dark. "Okay, keep your feet below your butt. Move right foot, good, push up, now left foot. That's it. Right, left, right, left."

To Jane's amazement, they actually did move upwards. Slowly, incredibly slowly, and she could already feel the strain in her legs and back and her arms were cramping and the dark pressed down on her, heavy, so heavy, and she couldn't let herself think like this, and so she searched for something else to think about, anything.

Dark. She smelled dust and dirt and humid air. Her body ached. No, don't think about that. The well's circumference stayed constant. The cribbing had changed, though. From what she could feel through her thick-soled boots, the wood was gone and the wall was now made of large stones, their cracks stuffed with clay.

But there was a limit to how much the well could occupy her thoughts when she could see nothing and feel only the pressure of the air above her head, Sandra's warm back, and pain.

She tried to fill her head with her figurine, and its enigmatic message.

No breastfeeding. Why not? Perhaps she was being silly to wonder, and the figure was just a puppet in a story. Pain shot up her shins and her thighs trembled, but she knew that if she gave up and fell, she'd cause Sandra's death, too.

No breastfeeding. In that case, what did the other hands mean? Did the one at the groin mean no sex? Did the hands clasped over the stomach mean no eating? No, that couldn't be right, there would be a hand over the mouth to indicate no eating. But maybe people in this culture didn't think the way she did.

Start over. No breastfeeding. Behind her Sandra was humming something perky to set their rhythm, the repetitive melody grating. She wanted to yell at her to be quiet. It wasn't really the song, though, it was the fact Sandra was happy enough, and had enough breath, to sing while Jane ached everywhere and flashes of dark jeering mouths kept appearing on the black well's walls, ready to laugh when the box flaps were sealed over her head.

If there was no breastfeeding, and the babies had no other source of milk, they would have died. Was that why this civilization ended, because the new generation all died? But that made no sense at all. Why would anyone starve their children? Perhaps the climate changed, grew warmer, and the heat addled everyone's brain.

Her brain was obviously addled. It was the weight of the space above her, pressing down, taunting her with how fragile she was and how arrogant to think she could overcome gravity. And the space below, so empty.

"How're you doing?"

Jane started, shocked by the intrusion of a voice into her black world. If she hadn't been wedged so tightly against Sandra, her involuntary twitch would have loosened her feet's grip on the wall.

"I'm okay," she said as cheerily as she could. "How about you?"

"This is fun. I wasn't really sure it was possible, and now I know it is."

Great. I'm doing something impossible.

"I'm feeling my abs, though," Sandra continued. "I should do more crunches."

Jane tried to think of a response. Talking was difficult, getting her lips to move and sound to flow through her dry throat. Then, as she pushed with her right foot to move her body up another scant millimetre, her foot cracked against something hard.

It was only reflex that saved her then, a recoil from the surprise that shoved her more snugly against Sandra.

"What is it?" Sandra asked.

"I hit something." Jane's words were wobbly but at least they came out.

"I wish I had an extra hand, so I could feel for obstructions. Can you step over it?"

Jane tried to pull one foot off the wall to probe how wide the obstruction was, but her other leg began to shake and the thought of trusting both their lives to just that one leg, not for the brief time of a step but while she explored the darkness with the other foot, was too terrifying. "I can't."

"It's all right." Sandra thought for a moment. "Here's what we'll do. We'll rotate, towards our left sides, got it? Very slowly.

And every couple of steps we'll try going up, to see if we've cleared the obstruction. I just hope it isn't a ledge of some sort going all the way around."

Jane hadn't considered that, and she was pretty good at thinking about worst-case scenarios. Then a spark of optimism poked its head out. "If it's a ledge, could it be right at the well's top?"

Sandra shook her head, her hair, dry now, brushing Jane's neck. "We haven't come nearly far enough. And we'd be smelling fresher air if it was. No, each society built on to the existing well. This group just didn't line up the new wall very well."

They took a couple of steps to the side, and tried going up. Jane's foot brushed something above. A couple more steps to the side. The obstruction was still there. Her heart plunged so far down that she imagined it must have dropped into the lake. Why did Sandra have to say they hadn't gone nearly far enough? They'd been in here forever, only Jane's trembling legs and aching back between her and blackness. I'm going to have to scream but if I do it will startle Sandra and we'll fall. The fear built up inside her, pushing on her chest, strangling her. And then she and Sandra tried another step up, and there was nothing in her way.

"It's gone," she said.

"Good. Onwards we go, then."

Onwards. Jane wondered if she'd wear the soles off her boots and they'd become too smooth to grip the wall.

She thought about breasts, and how it didn't matter what size they were, they could still feed a baby. She thought about the babies she might have someday. That reminded her of the

AIDS-12 babies she'd seen when she worked on an inner-city project in India. And suddenly the blackness of the well vanished, replaced with a flash of insight.

The dark came back, of course, no amount of mental brilliance could help her escape her current situation. Was it possible that the hands at the breast were indeed a warning? Of something worse, even, than starving?

"Poison," she said out loud. "The water is poisoned."

"Are you feeling something?" Sandra, for the first time, sounded just the tiniest bit worried. "A rash? Stomach pangs?"

Stomach pangs. That was it. "The figure," Jane said. "You know, my current jigsaw puzzle. It's a warning."

"Of what?"

"That the water brought death. It's not toxic to us, but their physiology was different. It probably affected babies first, since they're so tiny, through their mothers' milk. And other weak people, maybe the elderly, would have stomach pangs. The hand at the groin is meant to tell people not to have sex, not to have babies."

"Isn't that a bit overly dramatic?"

"All higher forms of life are gone. Just what would happen if toxicity built up through the food chain. As for what caused it, I don't know."

There was a brief silence while they continued to move up, step by painful step. Then Sandra said, "Some kind of disease?"

Jane shook her head. "No. There are relatively few diseases that can cross between so many species. And in terms of natural selection, a bacteria that killed all possible hosts would die out and wouldn't pass on its genes."

"The only other thing," Sandra said, "would be an environmental poison, then. But as far as we can tell, there's never been any technology on this planet."

"The technology must have come from somewhere else, then."

"Not from us, at least," Sandra said with a laugh. "We haven't had space travel long enough."

"But other races have," Jane said slowly, and then her left calf was seized with a sudden fierce cramp, and she yelped and without thinking tried to pull her arms out from Sandra's so she could massage the shrieking muscle.

"Sorry," she said and her voice wavered as she realized what might have happened, and she flexed her toe, pulling it towards her knee as far as she could, until the pain eased.

They continued on in silence. Jane wondered if even Sandra was getting tired, was admitting that maybe this climb was very slightly difficult. She didn't think so. Sandra still hummed, even though their step rhythm was so much a part of Jane now that she wondered if, assuming she actually got out of this well, she'd be able to walk normally. She tried not to listen, but that was difficult since sound echoed in the well, falling away below them, pushing up ahead. Jane focused on her body, afraid she was now tired enough that any distraction could cause a fatal slip.

And then, after another eternity or two, she realized the echoes of Sandra's song sounded different. *We've been here so long she's eroded her voice box.* A wisp of cool brushed her sweat-slick cheek. It took another brush before she realized what it was. A breeze.

Sandra started yelling, and suddenly light poured into the well, heads silhouetted against it, and Jane squeezed her eyes shut against the blinding light. She and Sandra were at the top of the well shaft.

Things happened very fast after that. Hands reached for their arms and legs and after a dizzying moment, Jane was able to let herself relax and trust them. She and Sandra were lifted out of the well and carried down the tel. Jane tried to stand but her legs, so long pushed with bent knees against the wall, refused to straighten.

The two women were put in beds in the infirmary dome and given glucose intravenously. After the doctor checked them over, their rescuers crowded around them, as Michael boasted about how he'd sounded an alarm when he couldn't find Sandra. She rolled her eyes at Jane, who understood the message about how Michael was so conceited he couldn't imagine Sandra not keeping their date, and Jane smiled. The smitten swains argued about who got to massage Sandra's legs, and the leftovers rubbed Jane's.

Sandra and Jane told their story, Sandra doing most of the talking, making their exploit sound like nothing more inconvenient than a light shower would be during a summer's day walk.

"You're so strong and brave," one of her swains said admiringly.

Sandra smiled. "No, I'm not. It was easy."

It wasn't easy. Not at all. And for the first time, now that her legs didn't ache as much and Jane thought she might someday be able to straighten her body again, the enormity of what she'd done swept over her. She'd been encased in the dark, and she'd moved up instead of falling.

"I am strong," she said out loud, and a couple of the swains glanced over, as if they'd just remembered she was there. They smiled and nodded and turned back to Sandra.

ꕥꕥꕥ

When Paul came to visit, Jane told him her theory about her figurine and what had caused the deaths and exodus from the peninsula. And some days later, once she and Sandra were fully recovered and back at work, Paul came to find Jane in Sherdville, where she'd put aside the figure for now since no more pieces had been found.

"We found your evidence," he said. "Someone dumped garbage here."

Jane nodded, her mind speeding. "Whoever did it probably assumed the primitive people living here wouldn't make a fuss, or couldn't do anything about the dump even if they didn't like it."

"The dump was where you thought," Paul said, "near the stream that feeds the underground lake. And with the garbage came alien microbes that polluted the water system."

Jane fitted two rough-edged pieces together that formed part of a bowl's rim, and used some FasDry to fill in the ragged gaps between them. "Have we identified the microbe?"

Paul shook his head. "The biologists are on it. But whatever it is, at higher concentrations it's definitely toxic to life here."

How sad, Jane thought later, as she and Sandra sweated in the gym dome. At least the people here would be remembered, through their buildings and bowls and beads. These things, buried for so long, were being brought to the light.

Jane brushed hair from her eyes.

"So," said Sandra. "How does it feel to be a superperson?"

"I wouldn't know," Jane said. "I like Batman better, remember." Then she added, with great certainty, "I am heroic enough to open a box." As Sandra stared at her, puzzled, Jane picked up the eighteen kilogram barbell. It felt as heavy as always.

The Loon's Tears

He travelled at night. He sought the light, but darkness had been his home for so long that he walked in shadow and didn't see the contradiction between his quest and his manner of seeking. The trees were thick overhead, their shadows deep and comforting. They eventually thinned, the darkness lifted, and moonlight glinted on water.

The man walked quickly. The water was black, the moon created silver streaks on its surface. Loons floated on the lake, small and rounded. One called, the sound wavering on the night air, and it spoke of distance and sadness and loss.

A wave whispered across the sand, lapped at his boot. A cry rose in him, but he strangled and killed it before it could leave his throat. He shook his foot, sending drops flying pale into the darkness. He shuddered, and hurried on.

The path followed the curve of the shore, then left to re-enter the forest and accompany a narrow river. He walked only a little way before the looming bulk of a mill tower told him he approached a village. The river gurgled beside him, passing between thatched houses, coursing down a steep drop, where it turned the millwheel before losing its laughter in a still, deep pool.

He entered the village as he did all places, stepping from the shadows, a piece of the dark detaching from the night and showing itself to be a man. His name was Devlin Rhobb. A tall man, broad and hard, dressed in the dusty clothes of one long on the road, the leather jerkin and sword-ready-at-the-hip of a soldier.

He intended to keep going, to pass through without leaving a ripple on the quiet surface of this sleeping town. He paused for a moment beside the silent pool, watching the millwheel turn, noting with expressionless surprise that the river entered the pool with no turbulence. The falling water vanished, swallowed by the smooth surface. At the far end of the pool the river escaped, continuing its course but subdued now, broader and stately. In between, the pool was sullen, dark with no reflections on its surface.

It was then the music caught him, tendrils wisping through the air to twine about his head, but it was her face that sprang the trap. High above him, she looked out from her square-framed window in the mill tower, her moon-round face glowing pale within her cloud of midnight hair.

She sang, her voice silver in the night. The sound entered Devlin's soul, filling the dark hollow inside him, not with light, but filling it all the same. He gazed up at the face framed in the window and knew he'd travel no further, not that night.

A rustle caught his ear, a rustle of cloth, and he lowered his gaze. A woman danced, clad in tatters and scarves, her arms swaying above her head. Her hair was long, black streaked with silver, and she flowed across the grass which ended abruptly at the silent pool. The only music was the song from the tower but Devlin realized that the music the dancer used to give life to her movements wasn't the music he heard.

There was a hiss from the tower window and the singer fell silent. Her gaze swept across the grass, deepened as she beheld the pool, then moved until it rested on him. His blood flared hot as their eyes met, then she drew her head back from the window and was gone.

The moon, three-quarters full, cast a gentle sad light. The woman danced, swaying to music only she heard. The grass glowed silver, but there was no reflection of the moon in the dark pool.

ഇഇഇ

Devlin returned to the forest to sleep, the window a dark pit in the tower wall, the dancing woman still flowing across the grass. He never slept in the open; even though he was a soldier no longer, old instincts die hard. And although the thought of sleeping at the base of the tower, the figurative feet of the moon-faced girl, appealed to him, there was something about the place that made him hesitate.

He didn't like water, hadn't since his youth, but this pool was dark and its depths perhaps hid clutching fingers. They reached for him, and he fled even as he felt the pull of the moon-faced girl.

ഇഇഇ

When he awoke the sun was high. He stretched and returned to the village. The mill tower seemed less tall by the light of day, its window framed with wood.

The village streamed with life, people driving goats or carrying goods, dogs running at their heels. They called greetings to one another. Birds swooped and soared overhead, their cheerful twitters filling the air. The people glanced at Devlin; a few nodded to him. Then one man, walking stooped with the aid of a stout stick, stumped across the grass by the pool.

Devlin expected the usual questions, where was he from and where was he going. But the man came up close, his faded blue eyes on Devlin's face.

"Mooning after her, are you then?" he asked, jerking his chin at the tower.

Devlin looked up, seeing in his mind the pale round face floating in its sea of dark hair.

"Heard her sing, did you?" the man continued. "She catches many with that voice."

"I'm not a fish to be caught," Devlin said, but his gaze clung to the window.

"There are many fish," the man said. "But none in this pool, even though there are plenty everywhere else in the river."

The blank window lacked the allure it had held during the night. Devlin realized the old man wouldn't leave him in peace. He'd dealt with men like this before, lonely, and so well known in the village that no one saw or heard them. They liked to talk and he'd used them to gain information about enemy numbers and movements, information they didn't know they possessed. "What is she called?" he asked.

"Hekate. Her father keeps her closed away in the mill. Her mother disappeared soon after she was born, and the father lives now in a bottle. Maybe he fears his daughter will leave, too."

"Poor girl," Devlin said, thinking of that beauty closed away from the world.

"Her voice is free," the man said. "It reaches far, and shines in many windows. Wives in this town are sure to pull the curtains firmly shut at night."

Devlin didn't like the thought that the moon-faced girl sang for other men. Her voice was a gift for him, and he'd be the man who set her free. "There was another woman last night."

"That would be the loon-lady." The man thumped at the grass with his stick, the green blades springing back after each blow. "Phoebe," he continued in answer to Devlin's questioning glance. "She's loony. Loon-lady. Get it?"

ഇഇഇ

Devlin went back that night. The moon shone overhead, and it seemed to be still three-quarters full. But that was impossible, and he gave it no mind.

Hekate sang at her window. He lay on the grass and lost himself in her voice. He saw the pale globe of her face, the black mist that was her hair, but didn't know if she was aware of him. Her gaze was always on the pool, or up into the night sky. He wanted to jump and shout, have her attention fall on him, but was reluctant to do anything that might cause her to stop singing. But then her song abruptly ended, and he sat up, blinking.

Phoebe danced in the silence of the night, her scarves swaying, and he thought of waves lapping at a sandy shore and loons bobbing on the surface of a lake. One called, just then, and she took the lonely sound and incorporated it into her dance. Hekate stood at her window, watching.

Devlin moved out from the shadow of the tower, onto the moon-washed grass. Phoebe wept as she danced; tears flowed down her cheeks and fell to the ground where they glowed for a long time before they faded. Her tears were all around her, shining in the grass, so it was hard to tell if she danced on the earth or in the sky, the stars glowing overhead, the tears on the ground.

He walked until he stood close to her, and as she danced about him her scarves brushed his hands and face. She seemed ephemeral, a creature of light and dew. He felt her warmth, though, heard her breath, and knew she was as real as he.

She tilted her head to one side as she studied him. He glanced back. Hekate was at her window. "Why does she stop her song when you appear?" he asked.

"Why do I dance to stop her song?" Phoebe's voice was high-pitched like the call of a loon. She swept into a spin, hair flying about her face. Her tears continued to fall and they lay at his feet, glowing silver. "Why do you speak to stop my dance?"

"Why does my voice stop your dance?"

"Your words are ugly." Her voice was fretful. "The sound blocks the song."

"The song stops when you dance."

"Not that song. The moon's song."

The moon hung large overhead. The pool showed no reflection.

"Why are you here?" the loon-lady asked.

"I seek the light."

She stilled her motion then, her eyes large and dark. "Have you found it?"

He shook his head.

"The light." Her lips caressed the words.

She made it sound as if he sought something bright and beautiful, not merely an end to the life of darkness he'd lived so long, a darkness which had nearly been his death. "I seek the light, but a song will do."

"If it's light you lack, you should continue your search and not tarry here."

He looked at the small window, the round pale face framed there. "Maybe she is light."

He heard a sound beside him, a cough or a choked-off sob. From the lake a loon call floated on the wind, sad and misty.

"I'm a creature of night and shadow," he told Phoebe. "A man of war. I've had enough of darkness now."

"There's darkness here. War and death are here, you've not escaped them."

Devlin lifted his head, drew in a deep breath as if seeking the scent of blood.

"Not that kind of death. But a grievous death all the same. The death of the moon's song." She began to sway, scarves flying about her thin body. The music was there, in her movements, in the sweep of her feet on the grass, in the sigh of the scarves, but Devlin heard only silence.

Her steps faltered, her arms drooped. Hekate began to sing, the sound silver-bright. Phoebe turned to Devlin. "She is not light. She swallows light and gives nothing back."

But he didn't hear her.

She sat on the grass and wept until the ground around her sparkled with her tears. The loon called again and Phoebe stood and drifted away towards the lake, but Devlin lay unmoving at the base of the tower.

ꙮꙮꙮ

During the day he stayed in the forest, hunting when he needed to eat, sleeping in shadow cast by sunlight. He went back to the tower when the sky was streaked with the dying blood of the sun. The moon was again three-quarters full. He was early, but Phoebe was earlier still, dancing across the grass, her scarves floating about her. The mill window was empty and dark.

"You are the pool," Phoebe said. She darted across the grass, her eyes reflecting the red in the sky. "A boy drowned in the pool once. Will I drown in you?"

Devlin shuddered. "Drowned?"

"A boy. Yes. Wanted the moon, he did. Cried for her, wept and howled for her."

She didn't move, and he could no longer see her clearly in the growing dark. The trailing ends of her scarves fluttered even though the air was still and heavy. "He wanted what all men want," she said, "that which is beyond their reach."

The pool lapped at its bank, its scent thick and damp.

"One night," she continued, "the boy saw the moon's reflection. It was a still night, and she shone silver on the pool. The boy forgot that to see the moon is to look up. He stared at her image and then dove. He passed through the reflection and disappeared."

Her voice stilled, no ripples left to disturb the night, and Devlin shivered. He forced out a laugh. “Maybe he found her after all.” He flung a hand towards the three-quarter moon. “Maybe he’s up there, serene in her bosom.”

Phoebe hissed, her eyes flaring red. “He cast himself down, not up. He was nothing. Only two have possessed the moon, only two held her and gave her what men give to women. Only two.”

He laughed again. “Gave her what?”

“Daughters,” she said.

Hekate began to sing. Devlin turned back to the tower. “I don’t want the moon. I want her.”

“I thought you sought the light.”

“The moon doesn’t lead to light.” In his mind he pictured again the dark lake, the silver path stretching between where he stood on the shore and the luminous globe of the moon. “I was a child, and believed I could touch all I perceived. I saw the moon’s path and ran out along it, but it didn’t hold me up. I fell into darkness. Wet fingers reached for me, icy voices called me. And I would have joined them, had not my father seen me in the lake and pulled me out.” He drew in a deep shuddering breath. “I have no love for the moon.”

“She has need of you.”

“Her need is nothing to me.”

“Just as your need is nothing to her.” Phoebe flung an arm toward the tower; her scarves floated up, too, then drooped back down.

“I can change that.” Devlin’s eyes were rapt on the window.

“You learned you can’t reach the moon. You tried and you failed, and yet you survived. That’s why she needs you now.”

"Why would the moon need a man, especially one such as I?"

"Why do so many men cry for the moon?"

Devlin had no answer.

"You could bring back her voice." Her breath wafted across his face, but it felt cold and its scent brought images of a lake, glowing beneath an evening sky.

"The moon has no voice."

"Not now. It was stolen from her."

"How?" He turned away to show he didn't care, but he already knew the answer.

"She took it."

He glanced back at Phoebe. Her eyes were fixed on the mill tower window, where Hekate leaned out, watching them. "You lie."

"A voice such as hers isn't natural. Its beauty is of the stars and the heavens. It can't come from one of this earth, not even from one such as her, one who is . . . "

He grabbed her arm, but his eyes were on the girl in the window. "One who is?"

"A daughter of the moon."

He released her arm, stared up at the moon-faced girl, then looked blindly at the pool.

"Why do you think her father hides in the tower?" Phoebe asked. "He possessed what other men can only cry for, for a short time only, but he held her. He wanted more than she could give, though. She gave him the most precious part of herself, a daughter, but he wanted more. When she left, he cast himself down into darkness."

"And Hekate?" Devlin asked.

"Hekate hates her mother for what she did to her father, and for what her father has done to her. He keeps his daughter locked in his darkness. But Hekate can look out, see her mother in all her beauty. Hekate sees no man but her father, but knows her mother's light reaches all places, all men. It makes what's ugly beautiful and banishes shadows."

"Hekate's song and beauty do these things, too."

"No. What Hekate does is only a pale reflection. One filled with hate can't bring beauty to others. But the pool which swallowed the boy loves the girl whose face is reflected on its surface every night. The moon was reflected there, too, and Hekate didn't want to share the only love she had.

"Hekate persuaded the pool to hide the moon's reflection, so only her own face could be seen. She called on the ghosts in the pool, the drowned boy, all the men who've cried for that which they cannot have. As the moon started to sing, Hekate seized the voice, made it her own, and gave it to the ghosts for safekeeping. The moon fled, weeping in silence. Since that day she can neither wax nor wane, and her voice is used by another."

Devlin looked at the three-quarter moon hanging among the glowing stars, then at the small woman surrounded by her glowing tears. He saw Hekate's pale face and dark cloud of hair and her beauty pulsed inside the dark hollow that was all that he was. He ran then, this man who was never afraid, he ran from the silver light of the moon that illuminated and laid bare all that it saw.

ꙮꙮꙮ

He found a place in the forest, a cave in the dirt beneath a towering tree, half dead, its roots dry above the soil. He wrapped his arms around his bent knees and squeezed his eyes shut. He remembered the only other time he'd lain hidden like this, but that time he'd hidden from the darkness that was death.

He led a charmed life, other men had said, a moon-kissed life. He spent his days eluding death, and never once had it even come close. He was a scout, walking ahead of the army, learning the enemy's whereabouts, his numbers, his plans.

He encountered beasts in the hidden dark places in which he walked, and overcame them all. He saw his quarry, the men of the other army, but they never saw him. He could make himself a part of the dark forest, turn himself into shadow.

It took both man and beast to bring Devlin down, a puma, black as night, distracting him from an enemy scout, whose arrow took Devlin in the stomach. He crawled to a cave, hid while both predators sought him. The puma found the man, and neither survived the encounter.

He'd lain in the dark for a very long time. He pulled the arrow from his body, filled the wound with leaves, lay in mud soaked by his own blood. When one day he awoke to sunlight streaming into his cave and realized he would live, he determined he'd live his life no longer in the dark. When he was well enough to travel, he set out to seek the light.

ꕤ

He slept now for a long time. When he woke, it seemed it had been night forever, for it was dark, and the moon shone overhead. He must have slept through the day, hunger and aching limbs told him that.

He looked up at the three-quarter moon, partially obscured by the trees. Instead of the unfilled globe, he saw a moon-round face surrounded by a cloud of dark hair. Without stopping to hunt and eat, he headed for the tower.

He burned for Hekate, his heart a red brand in his chest, his legs molten silver, barely strong enough to carry him. He stumbled through the forest, catching himself on tree trunks when he could, falling when he couldn't. Once in the village he moved more swiftly, the smooth ground easier to cross.

She was there, as he'd known she would be. He heard her voice first, when the tower was still too far away to make out her face in the dark. In all the houses of the village, the curtains were drawn tight across the windows.

He fell, panting, against the tower. He flung his head back and saw her face, pale and round, staring down at him. He put his hands flat against the wall and began to climb.

It was not easy. The stone was rough, but the cracks were narrow, the protrusions small. Still, he was an agile man, no scout could survive without that skill.

Her voice helped, twining about his limbs. And yet, when he reached the window, it was empty.

He pulled himself over the wooden frame and rolled to the floor, catching his breath. A table and two benches glowed orange in the occasional flicker from the banked cookfire. The top level of the tower had been divided into thirds by wooden partitions, and he saw two doors leading from this room. He darted to the one on his right.

It was a sleeping room. A man sat by the window, silhouetted by moonlight. The miller leaned his cheek on his fist, his elbow supported on the window frame. His other hand clutched a bottle. He never turned from the silver moon without.

Devlin spared no thought for him. He ran, his feet light, his body heavy with desire, to the other door and flung it open. She stood in the room, tall and serene, her body wrapped in a black cloak. His steps slowed. Her face grew larger as he neared, her eyes in shadow, no smile on her lips. He fell to his knees and clasped her legs. Her skin was warm and moist, and her scent, like that of a night forest, enveloped him. She took a step back and he let go and watched, still on his knees, as she moved until the backs of her calves brushed her bed of hay and linen. She parted the cloak, her skin glowing palely through the crack, and then pulled it fully open and let it fall in a black pool at her feet. Devlin reached for her, hands questing until they brushed the cloak, the bed, her foot.

It was small, the toes like little mushrooms beneath his palm. Her ankle was thin, his thumb and forefinger wrapped about it easily. Her skin was soft, the swell of her calf melted into his hand.

She sighed, the sound a misty cloud in the darkness, for her window faced away from the moon. She started to sing, the music wrapping him even as her arms took him into her embrace. He lost himself in her, sank deep, and darkness closed over his head. He emptied himself into her, prepared to be filled in return, filled with the light he sought.

She laughed, the sound low and cold as she rose from the bed. Alone, discarded, he stumbled after her, naked and shivering, down winding stairs into the mill room. This was the ground floor of the tower, one side of the rounded wall covered with shelves bearing sacks of grain, the rest of the room dominated by the huge stone grindwheel. Attached to the grindwheel was the wooden millwheel, only half visible above the hole in the floor it inhabited. It turned, paddles slick with water, and from below he could hear the roar of the river.

She stopped at the edge of the hole. He staggered, drunk from senses filled with her. She watched him and even his love-blinded eyes could see only amused curiosity and a touch of impatience on her round face.

He held out his arms, aching to possess her again. But as he reached her, she stepped to one side, out of his grasp, and he fell forward. He landed first on his knees, then sprawled on his chest at the very brink of the opening to the water below.

Hekate moved to stand by his head. Devlin could see only her bare feet and the empty space, his face splashed by an occasional flight of water from the torrent below. One shoulder hung over the drop, and his arm flopped down, his hand wetted by spray. "Not water," he sighed. She knelt, stroked his hair, her hand lingering on the side of his face, and then dug her knee into his side, rolling him into darkness.

He fell, naked, and the water closed over him. The voices were instantly there, the voices he'd heard as a child, heard still in his nightmares. Icy fingers caressed him, their touch lingering. He opened his mouth to scream and water rushed in, seeking to fill him.

Blackness within and without. A gurgling roared in his ears, but then he heard another sound. Thin and high at first, it grew louder, tugging at him, calling. Something brushed his arm, feather-light. The sound hung and wavered, spoke of sky vast overhead and water which, although deep and dark, was home. A loon, Devlin thought, and the cold fingers faltered in their grip. A feather touch caressed him, brushed the fingers away, wrapped him in warmth. He floated, the water now buoyant instead of sucking him down. He floated, he flew. Stars glistened overhead, and the moon watched.

When he woke, it was still night. A loon called, another answered. Sand gritted against his skin. He lay by the lake. The three-quarter moon rested heavy in the sky over the far shore, and between him and her glowing face, stretching before him, was her path.

Phoebe sat a little way from him, her bare feet washed by gentle waves. Loons stood on the sand beside her, white bands about their necks and white speckles on their wings glowing silver against their black feathers. A wave whispered across the sand, licked at Devlin. He scooted away from its wet touch. The sand beneath him was damp and water dripped from his hair. He sat up, drew his knees to his chest, wrapped his arms about them, and hung his head.

Phoebe placed one of her scarves, like a cloak, about him. He stood and she gave him another to knot about his waist.

"Twice now," she said, "you've sought the light and found only darkness. Now you must seek darkness, and in doing so you'll find the light."

He looked at the watchful loons flocked at her feet. "I don't need to seek darkness. I carry it wherever I go."

"That's why she needs you." The moon's path was a bright line moving restlessly on the black pulse of the lake. "Hekate has hidden the voice in a place of darkness. Only one who is of the night can travel there and hope to return."

Devlin looked out along the silver path, then down at his feet. The loons surged closer, their sharp-beaked faces turned up to him. "What care I about returning?" he asked. "What care I about the moon's voice? Light and song have betrayed me. They've been only yet another route to night, and I know enough of darkness without their aid."

As one, the loons moved to the water's edge, looked back at Devlin, swam onto the lake and dove. Devlin didn't move, staring at the now-empty lake. Then the loons resurfaced, still in a group, much farther out, having swum through the dark water and emerged into the light.

"You must go now," Phoebe said, and Devlin was startled to hear a voice.

"She used me," he said to the loons. "She emptied me of all I had and threw me away."

A loon called, the ululation reverberating in the night. Another responded, and another, until the air shivered with the high-pitched wails.

"Take the first step," Phoebe urged. She took his arm, led him to the edge of the moon's path, where water met shore. "Her time grows short."

"I'm nothing," Devlin said. "I don't exist. I'm a hole, a hollow."

Phoebe slapped his cheek. He put his hand to his face, stared at her.

"You're a man," she said. "You are not nothing. If there is a hole in you, it's of your own creation. Hekate did what all people do, thought of her own needs and not of those of others. As her father does. He is a man who's never known freedom. The loss of his own means nothing to him, and so the loss of his daughter's means nothing. But you are a man to whom freedom does matter."

She gripped his biceps and he put his hands on her back. The scarves and tatters of her gown didn't feel like cloth, they were stiffer and springier, and softer than any clothing he'd ever worn. He stepped back, slid his hands up to her shoulders, and saw in wonder she was clad in feathers. Black feathers, speckled with white.

"Do not hate Hekate," Phoebe said. "Our mother deserted us both. But while her father preferred to hide in his bottle, mine understood his lover's need for freedom. Her need spoke to his. He gave everything to me, freedom, the light, and the darkness, too."

"Our mother?" Devlin asked.

"We are sisters. Her father is the miller." A loon called out on the lake, and Phoebe glanced over, moonlight catching the lines of her cheek. "Mine is a loon. It's their music that fuels my dance."

He glanced over his shoulder. The forest was not more than ten steps away. He could reach it in an instant, lose himself in shadow.

"You don't wish to return to that life," Phoebe said.

He paused in mid-step.

"We're all made of light and dark," she added. "We find our own balance." The loon called again, its cry speaking of loneliness and loss, but then another answered, and another, and the cries merged together into a song of moon and water and open spaces which beckoned. “Take the first step. You’ll not be alone.”

Devlin looked out at the lake, saw the loons range themselves along each side of the moon’s path. “Loons are nothing to me. You’re nothing. The moon is nothing.” His throat tightened when he said the next words, but he forced them out. “Hekate is nothing to me. I’ve lived my life in darkness. Since I have nothing to return for, I’ll go.” He moved to the shore, where the waves glistened silver. Closing his eyes, he reached out with his foot. The water was cold and even though the fingers didn’t clutch at his skin, he knew they were there, waiting. He pulled his foot back, looked at Phoebe. “I don’t have my sword.”

Her smile was gentle. “You don’t need it. Where you go, weapons are not made of steel.”

He grasped at his hip, searching for the reassurance of the hard hilt, found only the filmy scarf. He faced the lake again, knew the voices chuckled in anticipation, knew the darkness waited. I am night, he reminded himself. I am darkness. He took a step, then another, this time with his eyes wide open.

The moon’s path supported him. Waves sent spray along his legs, but he did not sink. The loons stayed in their ranks on either side of him. He passed bird after bird, their faces all turned to him, red eyes watching, white spots glowing.

There was no transition. One minute he was on the water, washed by moonlight, the next, he was in darkness. Mist flowed about him, and indistinct shapes caught his attention, but when he faced them, there was nothing there. It reminded him of being in the forest late at night. He drew in a breath, seeking scents of green life and decay, he listened for the rustle that would not be leaves blowing, an animal scurrying, an owl floating on ashen wings overhead, but the step of an enemy. He'd come home.

Shadows ebbed and flowed about him. From somewhere very far away, he heard a song. Then he became aware of other voices, closer, whispers that were perhaps part of the mist, but perhaps not.

Something brushed his bare arm. He wheeled to search the darkness but all he saw was shadow, grey on black. Then came another touch, this time on his back, and another, sliding up his leg. The mist closed in.

"You are one of us," a voice hissed, the sound icy cold. Fingers ran up his arms. He steeled himself for the terror, remembering the same words and fingers from when he'd been underwater, drowning.

I am nothing, he reminded himself. I am empty. "You cannot entice me," he called to the faceless voices. "You have nothing to offer me. I have nothing already."

Hazy shapes materialized out of the gloom, hung in the fog, their edges indistinct. Devlin looked about, could see no horizon to this place, no end to the darkness.

"You are one of us." The hisses filled the space around him, coming from no one particular shadow but from all of them. "Why do you burden yourself with a body?"

"Am I one of you?" Devlin's eyes darted about, he took in all he could absorb about this place and these beings. They were the enemy, his job was to gain information that would help his army. He felt only a momentary fear when he remembered there was no army, no headquarters with warm tents and men to talk to, talk in real voices from bodies solid in the light. He'd never spent much time in those tents, but he'd known they were there. "Who are you?"

"You don't recognize us?" Smoky laughter oozed from the shadows. "You don't recognize yourself?"

"Show yourselves or speak your names." Devlin took a step forward. The music could still be heard, a voice silver-bright but still far away.

A shadow moved closer to him, took wavery form, showed itself to be a boy. "I am he who drowned in the pool," it said. "You know me, you touched my sorrow. You beheld she who was my betrayer, when you looked into the night sky. You have loved, you climbed the tower, you acted to take what you wanted, and you, too, were cast down into darkness. You are one of us. Why do you deny it?"

Other shadows pressed forward, took shape, beings who once were men. A shiver born of unseen ice colder than the water which had twice tried to claim him rattled inside his chest.

"We are," the shadows said, "the ghosts of men who cried for the moon."

"No man can have the moon." A thought formed in Devlin's head, but like the shadows it was hazy. He tried to focus on it, heard instead the music call to him. A loon's cry rose on the mist. He took a step, another. Shadows floated about him, appearing and vanishing, touching him with fingers that were not there. The song sent out tendrils, wisps that took hold of him.

The shadows wove about him more swiftly now, trying to push him back. He ignored them and moved forward, knowing not the direction in which to travel, knowing only where to go.

The song grew louder, more vibrant, more beautiful. The shadows wailed in the fog. Devlin's whole being was given over to the song, and it was a thousand times more beautiful than what he'd thought was the most beautiful thing he'd ever heard — Hekate's song. Hers had been a song only of herself, her sorrows, her yearnings. This was a song given freely to be heard by all. He moved through the fog, eager now, knowing he was very close. In the darkness ahead of him, a small light glowed like one of Phoebe's tears.

Something black and cold splintered, something encasing him in night shattered, fell to pieces and was gone. And he understood there'd never been a dark hollow inside him, he'd never needed to seek light to fill him. The night he carried was a shell he'd constructed. It had protected him from the darkness of his life, but it also kept out the light.

He reached out to the light, opened his eyes wide, his mouth, all his senses, and the song blazed forth, streaming past him. All about him the ghosts wept.

"No man can have the moon," he told them "You can bathe in her light for a little while, perhaps, but you cannot hold her. No man can look to the moon for light to fill him."

They closed about him then, their mist enshrouding him, their darkness seeking to cover him, but he strode through them, his head held high, his steps strong. "I am not one of you," he said. He walked farther, the darkness deepened, but he knew he would pass through it.

Later, he sat by the lake. The loons swam and dove, the moon shone overhead, a bit larger than three-quarter. Phoebe nestled against him, her warmth feather-soft. Devlin gazed out over the lake, and a space opened in his being. It opened, and light streamed out of him. Phoebe smiled and stood. She lifted her arms, her scarves floating on the night breeze. She danced, bathed in his light.

Vine

Daisy gave them whatever they wanted now. It was easier. If she resisted, they took it anyway, and then sometimes there were bruises or scrapes that she had to explain to her father. There were only so many times she could tell him she fell or bumped into the slide or jungle gym. She didn't play with the other kids, didn't hang upside-down or skip rope or throw the basketball through the hoop. During recess she travelled in her mind, and she liked it when they left her alone. Reading took her to places better than this world. Last year, in grade four, the class had an assignment to keep a list of all the books they read in one month. Daisy read thirty-two, way more than anyone else. The other kids hated her even more then, but she was used to them hating her. It was the way things were here.

This time they wanted the pink eraser shaped like a shell that her dad had just given her. She'd tried to cover it with her hand when she used it this morning, but someone must have seen it. She'd hoped she could keep it a bit longer. It wasn't that she loved it so much, but she was tired of making up stories for her dad about why her things went missing. Wordlessly, she held out the eraser on a flat palm.

Charlie snatched it, making sure she dragged her spike nails across the inside of Daisy's wrist as she did. She represented the *in* things this year, filing fingernails into a sharp point, and girls having boys' names. Charlie had been Charlene last year. Mary, now called Marv, saw the scratches appear on Daisy's wrist and, ever wanting to impress Charlie, grabbed Daisy's braid and yanked.

"Daisy," she chanted. "Poor little flower."

"Yeah," Harry, once Hanna, said, "little wilting flower."

"Flower's the name of a skunk." Charlie stood, eraser in her clenched fist. "Isn't that right, minions?"

Minions, that's what she called the girls who followed and flattered her. Daisy watched as Charlie dug her nails into the eraser and broke it apart into pink crumbs that she then threw at Daisy. A flame, unwise but unstoppable, heated her chest. "I'm surprised you know a word that long."

Charlie stared at Daisy, one hand flung out to indicate extreme shock. "It spoke," she cried, and the others gasped to show their shock also. "Skunks can't talk. Skunks only stink." Instantly the others pinched their noses and shrieked.

A group of boys wandered by to see what was happening. One of them was Jack, and Daisy knew that this was not going to end right away. She stared off to the side, where her vine hung over the green fence that enclosed the school yard, but Charlie's fingers gripped her chin and jerked her head around.

"I didn't give you permission to move, skunk," Charlie said. Jack sniggered and Charlie, emboldened, slapped Daisy across the cheek.

Daisy blinked to hold back tears at the sudden sting. "It's easy," she said loud enough for Jack to hear, "to pick on me, isn't it. You can't be so tough if the only person you're brave with is the bookworm."

Charlie's face reddened, and she kept her stiff back to Jack. Then she grinned. "Aw, I just beat up on wimps like you to pass time when there's nothing better to do."

That, Daisy thought, was probably true. The boys moved off and the girls turned to follow. Charlie, though, still stared at Daisy. "Nobody likes you," she said, her voice low and vicious. "Nobody wants you. Why don't you just disappear?"

ꕥꕥꕥ

Simon watched his daughter out of the corner of his eye as she ate her supper. Even though he'd imposed a no-reading-at-meals rule, her head was still bowed as if she looked down into a page, and her straight blonde hair fell forward to obscure her face.

She was so much like her mother. Lucie had read all the time, too, in high school where he'd met her, then, after they'd had to get married, in the apartment while she was growing Daisy. That's what she'd called it, growing a baby. She didn't like the word 'pregnant', said it was an ugly sound, nothing like the truth of what was happening to her. Simon didn't care what words sounded like, but he liked the names they'd chosen, Daisy for a girl and Birch for a boy, so calling it growing the baby seemed right.

"How was school today?" he asked, knowing she'd answer in one or two syllables but wanting to at least hear her voice. Sometimes he felt there was less of her here each day.

"Okay," she said without looking up.

"That new eraser work well?"

She did look up at that, her blue eyes as pale and distant as a hot summer sky. "It's great, Dad. Really great."

"They come in blue and green, too." The words tumbled out. "I could get you another one."

"That's okay." She looked back down at her invisible book. "One is all I need."

Simon decided then he would get her a blue one. A green one, too. It was a bit risky going back to Walmart so soon, but he could recognize plainclothes security people, and knew where the cameras were, so he'd be okay. A guy who worked security in an art gallery didn't make enough money to buy his daughter all the things the other kids had, but it did mean he knew how security worked and how to get around it. He'd do anything for Daisy. Anything that might make his girl, so quiet and pale, smile.

ຯຯຯ

As recess approached, Daisy watched the clock as eagerly as the other kids did. She raced outside as soon as the bell signaled her release and then, glancing around to make sure no one was looking, ran to where her vine hung over the tall green fence.

There were lots of vines on the other side. This one tendril, though, had left the company of others like itself and had grown over the fence top so it could explore what was on this side. The schoolyard here was usually less crowded during recess, because it was away from the basketball hoop and the painted hopscotch grids. Maybe Charlie and the others would find something more fun to do than pick on Daisy.

She lifted a hand and brushed the length of the vine, caressing the soft leaves and tough wiry stem. Where would she go today? To Narnia, where she'd walk with her hand tangled in Aslan's mane? A gust of wind blew, and the vine swayed back and forth. Daisy tugged gently on it and was instantly on the deck of a ship. Ulysses' ship, and he was beside her, lashed to the mast, struggling against the ropes as the Sirens' song called to him.

"Be strong," Daisy told him, and he turned to her, as if a spell had been suddenly broken. "I'm here for you," she said. "Be strong like me."

Then, as the song faded into the distance and Ulysses told her how he'd never have survived the Sirens without her, something scraped against the side of the ship. Running to the rail, she saw Rat and Mole in their rowboat. "Come with us to the river," they called, and she leaped from the ship rail and landed in the boat.

"I'd love to come with you," she told them, "but we have to keep a watch out for Peter Pan, because he begged me to go flying with him today."

The vine twined about her wrist and she blinked at it, and turned away to see that almost all the other kids were already back inside. She must have missed the bell. Charlie stood a little way from her, flanked by Harry and Marv.

"Are you deaf as well as stupid?" Charlie called, and giggling, they raced into the building.

Daisy followed, one slow step after another.

Simon slipped on his jeans and put his uniform into the small locker. These days he was usually the only staff person here. The gallery was small, three rooms with plain white walls that were covered with an ever-changing array of modern art. The owner was a rich woman whose husband bought her the gallery as a present when she had wanted to Be Somebody in the art world. That's what she'd said when Lucie had brought Simon over to be interviewed for the job. Be Somebody. You could hear the capital letters as she spoke.

Before she started growing the baby, Lucie had talked about university. She and Simon would work a year or two after high school to make money, and then they'd go together. Simon had never thought much about what he'd do after school. No one in his family had ever gone to university. No one in Lucie's family had either, but she'd always had big dreams. Her dad kicked her out when Daisy was a bud inside her, and so she and Simon moved into the apartment where he still lived. He went to work, arriving early to open up, staying late to lock the doors, making sure no one touched the paintings in between.

The owner was now wanting to Be Somebody in the dance world, but she kept the gallery, and appeared for show openings where she walked around holding the artist's arm and smiling at everyone. During other times, if someone wanted to buy a painting, Simon had a stack of cards to hand out with the owner's name and phone number.

Simon took the bus to Walmart, smiled vaguely at the greeter, and headed down brightly lit aisles towards the school supplies. He wondered if he should apply for a job here. He didn't mind the gallery, but sometimes certain paintings reminded him so vividly of Lucie that his chest hurt. The ones there now were huge, filled with swooping lines in bright colours. He'd seen the artist, a tiny skinny woman dressed in yellow, waving a cigarette about.

She'd read all the time during the growing of Daisy, school books because she was finishing grade twelve by correspondence, and other books, too, even after she finished the courses. She read to newborn Daisy, a book in her hand, as she stood by the stove stirring a pot and rocking Daisy before putting her to bed.

She told Simon about the books, the places they took her, the people she met. She wanted him to read some of them and he tried, but he'd never been one much for reading, and he preferred to watch TV.

Lucie read all the time until the day, when Daisy was two, she came to him, crying, stammering she was sorry over and over. When he eventually got her calmed down, she told him she'd applied to universities, and had got a scholarship at one, so she could go right now, today. It wasn't that she didn't love him and their baby, but she needed a bigger world to live in. Simon wasn't sure what she meant. There was only one world, Earth, as far as he knew. He also wasn't sure what was wrong with their life; they were happy together, they had a beautiful baby girl. But he'd helped her pack her clothes and watched, holding Daisy in his arms, as she walked out the door.

It was just him and Daisy then. His parents were dead and he'd been an only child. He answered Lucie's letters, pages filled with words he didn't understand and experiences he couldn't visualize. She never asked about Daisy. Six months later, divorce papers had arrived by mail.

There were books in the school supply section, some for reading, others for writing in. Simon knew a book was more likely to make Daisy smile than another eraser, but he hated books. Books were the reason Lucie had left him, they'd made her dissatisfied with the life they'd had. He'd do nothing to encourage this bad habit Lucie'd passed on to Daisy.

The other people around him were all shoppers. None of them had the walk or the face of security. He put two erasers in his pocket, took a pen, too, one that wrote in sparkly purple ink. Surely that would bring a smile to her eyes. He didn't feel guilty about doing this, not any more. Yes, it was wrong to steal, but it was more wrong for his daughter to be so pale and sad.

As he was leaving, he noticed a rack of T-shirts that said "Designs by Dave" on the front. He'd seen other girls wearing shirts like this the days he'd surprised Daisy by meeting her after school. They were expensive, even though you'd think anything with advertising on it would be cheaper.

He couldn't afford to get Daisy the clothes the other kids wore. Not when shoes cost more than a hundred dollars. He'd explained this to her, and she'd told him that it was okay, she didn't care what she wore, it wouldn't make a difference to anything anyway. He got the impression that she didn't have many friends. She talked about other kids if he asked, but she never went to a friend's house or had anyone over. Maybe if she had one of these shirts she'd fit in better.

He'd never stolen anything like this, though, too big to fit in a pocket. He picked one out, slipped it off its hanger, stood considering how best to do it. Someone brushed a rack behind him, set hangers jangling. Simon turned, saw a heavy-set man in jeans and sneakers. Security. Simon smiled, wondered if he could afford the shirt if he did without lunches for the next week, remembered that Daisy needed new shoes. She was growing so fast. He hung up the shirt and left the store. Maybe if he brought a bag or something next time, he could get her a shirt.

೩೩೩

The hobbit danced through the trees, waving his little sword, singing "attercop" at the spiders. Daisy danced, too, singing "Itsy-bitsy-spider" which she knew would make them mad because they were so big. She and Bilbo had already saved the dwarves from the trolls, and now they would save them again from the spiders.

Suddenly Bilbo whirled to face her. "Where are you?" he yelled.

Spiders and dwarves fell from the trees, landing with sad plops, and she looked up to see her father standing over her. "Where are you?" he repeated, his voice even harsher, his face red. "You're reading, but then you aren't, I can tell because your eyes don't move but you still look into the stupid book." He dropped to his knees in front of her and put his hand on hers where it held the book. "Please," he said, and now his voice was quiet. "Where do you go?"

His hand was tight, and his eyes were so close that he looked like the Cyclops in Ulysses, and she didn't know what to say.

"You have to tell me what's going on," he said. "You have the right clothes now, and I got you the iPod. You have all this great stuff to keep you here. Why do you go away?"

She knew the answer to that. "It's better there."

His hand gripped hers painfully for a moment, then he flung it from him, stood up and swore. "Books," he said, glaring at her. "Books took her from me, and now they're taking you. Do you know that sometimes when you're reading but you're not, you move so far away from me that I can almost see the pattern of the chair right through you?"

Daisy didn't laugh, although the idea of the pink and blue upholstery flowers shining through her was pretty silly. Her dad wasn't laughing.

"Come on." He grabbed her arm, yanked her to her feet. "Put on your shoes and coat."

Her shoes were new, canvas runners with velcro. She knew her dad thought she wanted a different brand but she really didn't care. Any shoes were fine, as long as they didn't pinch her feet. She knew, too, that if she had wanted the other shoes, her dad wouldn't have had enough money, and then he would have been sad. She wondered sometimes how he had money for the designer clothes. Maybe it was because he'd bought those that he didn't have enough money for expensive shoes.

Once they were outside, he held her arm and hustled her along the sidewalk. He moved so fast she had to run. "Where are we going?" she asked, but he didn't answer. After a few blocks, she recognized the route. They were going to the gallery. She liked it there, and hadn't been for a while. But why was Dad taking her now, and in such a hurry?

They arrived at the square white building jammed in between taller buildings. Dad pulled her up the concrete steps and fumbled for his keys. His hands were shaking and he dropped them. They both bent to pick them up but Daisy, because she was shorter and had less distance to bend, got them first. He took them without looking at her, jammed one in the lock, and pushed her through the open door.

She stood in darkness, heard his footsteps on the wooden floor as he moved away from her. She didn't feel alone because the dark was filled with light. That was a funny thing to think, she knew, but it was what she felt. Then Dad reached the light switches, she heard a click, and suddenly colour and movement leapt out at her.

She drew in a deep breath and let it out slowly. Joy bubbled in the nearest painting and danced until it was inside her, too. Lines of yellow swooped up and down, and at the top they ran over the frame and onto the wall above. Orange and red lines supported the yellow ones, helping them to reach for the top, cheering when the yellow broke through. One red swoop sagged near the bottom, almost breaking through the frame there, but a yellow one was sliding down towards it, to help it before it fell. She sighed with pure happiness and reached out to the painting, stopping just before her fingers brushed the canvas.

"You like it, don't you," Dad said from beside her. She nodded.

"I do, too." He was silent for a moment. "And I hate it." The words burst out of him, and she glanced up, startled. "I love it and I hate it," he continued, "because these paintings are so like your mother." He brushed the knuckles of one hand across his face, and she was surprised, and scared, to see tears glinting in his eyes.

"Dad." She held her hand out him, but he didn't see it, was turning jerkily from one painting to the next.

"She was filled with colour. And dreams." He pointed to another painting where the colours broke through the frame. He turned back to Daisy, took her face between gentle hands. "She left me because of books. And you're leaving me, too, because of books." He took in a shuddering breath. "It's different, she became more and more colourful before she left, while you are paler and wispier every day. But you both left me. I want to take every book I see and tear it into shreds. But I can't." His hands fell away from her, and he looked down to where they hung loosely at his sides. "You both love them so much, I can't destroy them."

Daisy didn't move, hardly dared breathe. Dad sank to the floor, almost collapsing, and she sat beside him. "Why," he asked, "do you both have to leave me?"

She opened her mouth to answer, but the gallery door opened and closed with a sharp click. A woman stood in shadows there, for her dad had only turned on the lights that illuminated the paintings, and the entry hall was dark.

Her dad sat up straighter, and then stood. "Lucie?" He opened his mouth to speak again, but for a long moment, nothing happened. "Is it you?"

The woman stepped forward, and while this woman had blonde hair like the photos of her mother that her dad had kept, she was much smaller and thinner. Dad sighed, and as the air left him it was if he was deflating, losing all that held his pieces together.

"You like to come here at night, too?" the woman asked.

"This is the artist," Dad said dully to Daisy. "She created all these paintings." Daisy took his hand. His fingers were cold.

"I have to come back," the artist said. She was dressed in green, green leggings, a long sweeping green tunic, a green band around her head. "New paintings are growing inside me, but I have to come back to where I was the last time I grew something. I broke through the frames—where do I go now?" She turned in a slow circle, panning across her work, and then walked into the next room, filled with more of the colour and movement she had grown and brought to life.

Dad looked at where Daisy held his hand, stared as if he'd never before seen two hands with their fingers intertwined. She tugged at his until he bent and his head was beside hers. "It's not you," she said, her breath a sigh against his ear. "It was never you." She led him out of the gallery and took him home.

ꕥꕥꕥ

Daisy was tired at school the next day, because she'd gone to bed late. At recess, she stood by her vine, idly tugging on it, but without the energy needed to join her friends waiting in other worlds. But she heard laughter, and a brown furry head poked over the top of the fence and grinned at her. "Curious George!" she cried. She hadn't seen him for a long time. He held her vine out to her, and soon the two of them were swinging across the jungle, leaping from one vine at the end of its arc and catching the next. Then they heard a call from the ground below. It was Babar the elephant, who wanted to play, too. He took hold of a vine with his big round foot, and jumped into the air. Curious George laughed so hard at the sight of the elephant swinging through the air.

Something sharp scraped her forearm, and she fell from her vine, landing on the asphalt of the schoolyard. Charlie's hand was still on her arm, but there was no blood, no red welts from the pointed nails.

Daisy stared at her, knowing Curious George and Babar were still with her. "I don't want you to hurt me anymore."

Charlie made a fist. "Tough." But instead of hitting Daisy, she grabbed the vine and yanked, tugged harder, finally dug her feet in with all her weight until it broke at the top, right where it came over the fence. Charlie fell backwards and lay sprawled on the ground, the vine curving over her, its ends trailing on the asphalt.

Daisy stared at the empty place on the fence, then at the broken vine. Tears rose, hot in her eyes. Something broke inside her, and it hurt, but as well as feeling pain, she was glad. Now she had no roots to keep her here.

She stood, and Charlie peered closely at her face to see if she was crying. She smiled to see tears and jabbed viciously at Daisy's stomach. Her fist passed through Daisy, thudding hard on the fence. Charlie cried out in pain.

"What happened?" Marv asked, and Harry glared at Daisy.

"She must have moved out of the way." Charlie stood, sucking her knuckles, her eyes never leaving Daisy's.

Daisy looked down to where her vine lay, flat on the asphalt, already smaller and thinner. "You won't hurt me ever again," she said, and lifted her chin. Her pen stuck out of Charlie's pocket, the one that wrote in sparkly purple ink, and she took it back.

ഇഇഇ

Simon quietly opened the door to Daisy's room. There was not enough of a bump beneath the cover for a child to be in the bed, but her even breathing filled the air. He closed the door, returned to his chair in the living room. She travelled in her sleep, he knew, as well as during the day, visiting other places. Some worlds were kinder than this one, and some weren't, but he had to let her explore them by herself.

It wasn't him that Lucie and Daisy left, he knew that now. They just had other places to travel to, and he'd been afraid to let them go. Lucie was gone, but somewhere, surely, one of her roots was still entwined with one of his. Maybe he'd ask her father for Lucie's phone number and call her. Perhaps she could help him with Daisy.

He picked up a book that lay on the end table beside him. It was called *Peter Pan.* As he laid it in his lap, it fell open to a page partway into the book. He started reading, absorbing each printed word.

Come fly with me Peter crowed. Daisy sat up in bed to see Peter hovering outside her window. *Come fly* he cried again, and she smiled.

Simon smiled, too, and turned to the front of the book so he could read the story from its beginning.

Oh, Won't You Wear My Teddybear

Andrea heard a rustling in her bedroom. The sound brought her bolt upright, sheet crumpled in white-knuckled fingers, her breath tight in her throat. Had someone broken in? Maybe if she didn't turn on the light, he wouldn't notice she was there.

Don't be a fool, she told herself. There's no one here. And even if there was, you're in no danger. You're the invisible woman, remember? She reached out and flicked on her bedside lamp.

No prowler dressed in stripes and a mask, carrying a bag marked "LOOT." The rustling continued, and it came from the floor.

She looked down. A very fluffy hamster, fur trailing from its backside in two long wisps, waddled out from under a plastic bag she'd tossed in the corner.

Andrea shrieked, and then felt foolish. How could anyone be afraid of something so cute? She encountered disturbing and horrifying sights every day at work, and dealt with them with equanimity. Yesterday she'd autopsied a car crash victim, determining that it was a heart attack that sent his car spinning off the road and into a tree. Exploring his broken body had not heightened her breathing or caused her blood pressure to rise. Apparently it took a small furry animal to send her adrenaline surging. She released her grip on the sheet. "What are you doing here?" she asked the hamster.

It sat up on its hind legs and looked up at her. She bent over, put out her hand, and it hopped onto her palm.

The hamster, a female, had black fur, a pointy nose, long whiskers, and black caviar eyes. She was disgustingly cute. "I think I'll call you Jasmine," Andrea said. Jasmine sniffed the air, her nose moving up and down, up and down. Her furry stomach pressed into Andrea's hand, soft and warm. Andrea smiled, the warmth spreading through her, as if she'd pulled a favourite old blanket up over her body. She lay down and went to sleep as Jasmine roamed her bed, exploring.

When Andrea woke at her usual time, seven, there were two hamsters in her bed. The new one was tan-coloured, and Andrea named him Spot. "I guess you were lonely," she said to Jasmine. "It must be nice to want a friend and have one just appear."

She got up, pulled off her nightgown, and went to stand in front of her mirror. Carefully, missing no part of her body, she examined her skin for signs of cancer. She ran her fingers along one arm, gently rubbing the mole just below her elbow, checking if it was larger or if its texture had changed. She twisted her head, looking over her shoulder at her bare back in the mirror, at the wine-stain birthmark. It was no larger than the day before. There were no new marks on her face, her hands, her legs. She rotated her shoulders, took in deep breaths, and relaxed, ready to face another day. She dressed in her greens and ate cereal for breakfast. A new hamster had joined the others, this one a lovely white and tan brindle. He was even more fluffy than the others.

Still, cute as they were, Andrea did wonder where the hamsters were coming from. She went through the ground floor of her house, checking baseboards on the external walls, examining the fit of the front and back doors, looking for holes or cracks large enough for a hamster to fit through. She found only dust. There were no openings to the outside world. She watched the hamsters skitter across her kitchen floor, got out her list of things to do that day and added, "Buy cage and hamster food."

She put on her lab coat and slung her stethoscope around her neck. She almost never used it, as her job involved analyzing bits of people and she rarely dealt with a whole living person, but she wore it because other people in the hospital recognized it as a badge of office and treated her with more respect.

ണണണ

Her weekly quilting bee was that evening, and she looked forward to telling her friends about the hamsters. There'd been five when she got home from work, and she worried about whether the cage she bought was too small. She poured cedar shavings on the cage floor, added the food bowl, attached the water bottle, and looked about to see six hamsters watching her with great interest.

"Where are you coming from?" she asked. The six stood up on their hind legs, front paws in the air, and looked at her. She smiled. "It doesn't matter, does it. You're here."

They readily allowed her to pick them up and put them in the cage, where they rooted about in the shavings. One of them started chewing on a cage bar, and she saw with admiration that he had long curved teeth. She sighed at how cute the hamsters were, and got out her quilting bag.

"I have hamsters," she told the other quilters. They sat around a huge quilt frame. The quilt top they'd pieced together over the past weeks was done now, and they were sewing together the top, the batting, and the backing, using their needles to quilt in a pattern of whorls and swirls. The colour design was one of sun and sky, with bird silhouettes flying across the blue, and a border of leaves all around the edge. It was supposed to be what a person would see if she lay on her back in the centre of a circle of trees and looked up into the sky.

"They're teddybear hamsters," Andrea added, proud of the knowledge she'd gained at the pet store.

"I didn't know you were into pets," Marlene said. She had seven cats and three dogs, and was proud of being an animal person. "When did you get them?"

Andrea had to stop and think. "I didn't get them. They just appeared."

Edna and Lucinda looked at each other, eyebrows raised. "Andrea," Edna said hesitantly, "you know it's not exactly normal to have hamsters just appearing."

"I like them," Andrea said, feeling defensive. "They are welcome at my house."

"Be careful." That was Jane, who owned the house they were in. The bee always met in Jane's house because she had a room big enough for the quilt frame. It was the cleanest house

Andrea had ever seen. "Hamster infestations can be terribly hard to get rid of." Jane sniffed. "Have you again left cookie crumbs in your living room sofa?"

Andrea wasn't sure if Jane was joking or serious. It was often hard to tell with her. She moved her needle up and down, up and down, through the quilt. "I just cleaned my sofa. And you should see them. They're so soft and warm."

"Whatever turns you on, honey," Lucinda, tall and muscular, looked around, accepting the laughs coming her way.

Andrea wrinkled her nose. "Maybe I need that in my life. There's no fluff or warmth where I work, after all. In the morgue, no one is cute or cuddly."

There was a silence, broken only by the small pops of needles puncturing fabric. Then Lucinda grinned. "Sweetie, you have friends. You telling me I'm not fluffy?"

They all laughed. "Who's coming to my party this weekend?" Lucinda asked.

All the women except Andrea said they were. It was spring, the start of party season. Each of the quilters was divorced or had never married. Andrea, at forty-four, was the oldest.

"I don't know," she said. "It seems that every party I go to, all I do is talk to all of you."

"And what's wrong with that?" Edna stopped sewing and put her hands on her hips.

"Nothing." Andrea ran out of thread, tied a neat knot, and pulled it through the top into the batting. "It just seems that if we're at a party where there are other people, we should talk to them."

"Other people?" Marlene laughed. "You mean men."

"Men don't notice me." Andrea squinted at her needle and slid a new thread through its eye. "I'm invisible."

Lucinda punched her lightly on the shoulder. "You seem pretty solid to me."

"Men see what they want to." Andrea shrugged. "They look for cute and perky and if what's there is wrinkled and saggy, they see nothing."

"Oh, don't get on that kick." Edna, sitting next to Andrea, put her arm across her shoulders and gave her a hug. "You're an attractive woman. Maybe you need to do something to get them to notice you. Wear bright colours or something."

Andrea looked about the circle, at the faces of her friends. Each one was vivid, each beautiful in her own way. Marlene, all sharp planes and angles, high cheekbones, arching brows. Lucinda, large and strong, had a smile that, if you got it at close range, made you feel you'd been kissed by an angel. Edna, so pretty with her red hair and huge green eyes you wanted to hate her, but you couldn't. And Jane, her dark eyes so intense it was hard to talk to her one on one.

"I tried being noticed," she said. "I wore a red feather boa over a black and pink dress, and I had a black hat with a peacock feather on it."

"I remember that outfit," Lucinda said. "I loved it."

Jane wrinkled her nose. "You're not supposed to love an outfit like that. You're supposed to notice it."

"It didn't work," Andrea said. "Nobody noticed me. Older women are invisible, just like I told you. It doesn't matter what we wear. You'll all find out, when you're as decrepit as me."

No one said, "You're not decrepit." Andrea hadn't expected them to. They all cared too much for one another to say the expected.

ॐॐॐ

When Andrea got home she found thirteen hamsters playing under her living room furniture and, judging from the rustles in the kitchen, a few more in there had discovered her paper recycling box. Some were sleeping, piled together in a corner of the sofa, a fur ball coloured brown and orange. The cage, its door firmly shut, stood empty.

Questions knocked against her skull, demanding to be noticed. The number of hamsters was increasing for no apparent reason, just like the cells in a tumour, a melanoma, perhaps, growing with its own logic, its own purpose. She shivered and wrapped her arms about herself. Three hamsters discovered her feet. One was Jasmine, and she climbed onto Andrea's shoe and stood up on her hind legs, looking up as if trying to find her face. Andrea bent and scooped her up, pressing the soft fur against her cheek. "You can't be a cancer. You're too cute." She picked up the empty cage and put it in the back of her hall closet.

Andrea switched on her TV. It was tuned, as usual, to the Weather Channel. She stroked Jasmine and the other hamsters who were congregating on her lap, and waited for the Ozone Hole report.

The satellite image appeared on her screen, coloured a cool blue where the ozone layer was thick and complete, gradually shading through purple to a fiery orange to show the hole. "Over Antarctica," the weatherman said, "ozone protection is ten percent of normal." The graphic shifted, its motion swift and sudden, leaving Andrea feeling as if she'd just flown through an air pocket. The continent shape beneath the blue was now the familiar full bosom and narrow waist of North America. "Over the North Pole," the weatherman continued, "the ozone layer is thinning, the hole's edge brushing northern Canada, here and," he used a red laser pointer, "here."

Andrea tucked her legs up beside her on the couch, sending three hamsters tumbling from her chest to her lap. "Ultraviolet," she told Cherry, a fat ochre hamster who was grimly climbing back up, "is not good for hamsters and other living things."

Cherry curled up on her shoulder and went to sleep. Spot and another hamster, she thought it was Fido but she wasn't sure, as there were by now seven orange hamsters, arrived on her lap. She told them, "We are killing our planet's skin and there's nothing I can do about it." Spot and maybe-Fido sat up and looked at her, their round black eyes unblinking. "I'm scared."

Spot climbed up to her shoulder. He stood on his hind legs and balanced his front paws against her cheek. His tiny claws pressed against her skin, the touch oddly soothing.

The next morning, after Andrea checked herself for signs of skin cancer and found no changes, she arrived at the hospital and discovered that Jasmine had come to work with her. The hamster clung to her lab coat, a ball of fluff just above the breast pocket, her nose whuffling up and down, up and down, as she took in the new scents in the air. Dr. Baines, one of the other pathologists, passed Andrea in the hall leading to the lab. "Nice brooch," he said.

ᘐᘐᘐ

Andrea decided to go to Lucinda's party. "I can't just give up," she told Spot. Rover and Tibby sat on her shoulders, listening, too. "I don't mean to insult you," she continued, "you're wonderful company, and so cute, but I need human company. Maybe even male company." At her feet, other hamsters wandered about, sniffing her shoes, exploring under the furniture. She thought there were thirty-seven of them now, but she wasn't sure.

She put on a black velvet skirt and a raspberry-pink silk shirt, brushed her shoulder-length dark hair back from her face, and set off for Lucinda's. Rover and Tibby had resumed their posts on her shoulders. Walking into Lucinda's loft apartment, they stood up to take in the new sights, each placing a paw on her earlobe for balance. A man she knew slightly, who worked with Lucinda in Emerg at the hospital, complimented her on her earrings.

All about Andrea, people mingled, talking, eating, laughing. Colours swirled, merging from one pattern to another like a kaleidoscope. Most people seemed to be about her age or a little younger. Across the room Edna smiled and waved. Jane and Marlene stopped to talk on their way to the kitchen for fresh drinks. Other people brushed by her as if she didn't exist. Andrea wondered when she'd be invisible enough for them to walk right through her, a woman without substance as well as without an outer surface.

The hamsters were warm and soft against her neck. She scanned the room, looking for a likely prospect, determined to take matters into her own hands. A little way from her, sitting on a couch, was a man wearing a blue-striped shirt.

He had a thick black mustache and his eyes reminded her of a policeman's, watchful but shuttered, taking in but letting nothing out. The place next to him on the couch was empty, and she thought he looked lonely.

She sat down beside him. "Hi. My name's Andrea."

He looked blankly at her, then back at the knots of people.

Press on, she told herself. Keep shooting until you see the whites of their eyes. "How do you know Lucinda?"

Another man came to the couch. The man she was talking to jumped to his feet, punched the new man on his arm, and the two of them merged into the crowd.

Andrea took Tibby from her shoulder and stroked his brown and orange fur. "What do you think?" she asked. "Try, try again?" Tibby butted his nose into the space between her thumb and forefinger. She took that to be a yes.

A man stood by the window, one shoulder against the wall. His hair was long, tied at the back of his neck by a leather thong. Andrea liked ponytails on men.

"Hi," she said. She propped her hip against the windowsill. "I'm new in town and I don't know anyone. Can I talk to you?"

The man's gaze went to her face, then moved past it to over her shoulder. A smile grew on his face, and he reached to take the hand of a young woman approaching him from behind Andrea. The two moved away, talking animatedly.

Andrea held both hamsters against the front of her neck, closing her eyes and revelling in the feel of fur against the skin under her chin.

"I'm lonely. Talk to me." The man she said this to asked her if she knew where the bathroom was and, when she pointed him in the right direction, moved on without a further word.

She sat on the couch again, between two men. One drummed his fingers incessantly on his thigh, the other slouched back, his head tipped so he stared blankly at the ceiling. "I may be old," she said to the ceiling gazer, "but I'm a nice person. Would you sit and have a drink with me?" He ignored her.

She turned to the finger drummer. "I may be old, but I'm a nice person. Would you sit and drink Geritol with me?" He jiggled the glass he held in his other hand so the ice cubes rattled, tossed back the rest of his drink, and stood up to head for the bar.

Andrea wandered into the kitchen and talked with Edna for a while, about the quilt, the hole in the ozone layer, the latest group of med students she'd taken through the morgue, and the artist who'd had a tantrum at the gallery where Edna worked, because his paintings were hung six inches lower on the walls than he'd wanted. Then she thrust back her shoulders, puffed out her chest, and went back into the party.

She walked to a man standing alone, tapping his foot to the Dire Straits music. They both watched in silence for a moment at the people dancing, and then Andrea touched him lightly on his shoulder. He looked at her, startled.

"I've just learned I have a terminal brain tumour and will die tomorrow," she said. "I've never slept with a man, and it's an experience I want to have before I depart this world of tears forever. Will you — ?"

A look of intense fright came over his face, and he scuttled away, looking back over his shoulder once, eyes wide, his skin pale.

"I've made progress," she told the hamsters. "He noticed me." She stuck out her tongue at the retreating man, then went to find Lucinda to say goodbye.

At home again, she turned on the Weather Channel. The ozone hole over Antarctica, she learned, had increased slightly. Scientists were unsure of why this happened, and two men and one woman who worked for the Weather Bureau debated whether the growth of the hole was an anomaly due to unusually active sunspots, or if it was the beginning of a trend which proved that human awareness of the effects of pollutants, and a genuine desire to save the planet, would have no effect.

"The hole in the sky," Andrea told the eight hamsters on her lap, the three on her chest, and the one on the top of her head, "is real. People can't see it so they pretend it's not there. They don't want to deal with it. People think if they pretend something doesn't exist, it will go away. It's easier than controlling pollution. Or seeing the person beneath the wrinkled face." She paused, stroking the hamsters. "But don't worry. I won't let you get skin cancer."

The hamsters stirred, their small claws gripping her clothing, their noses snuffling against her skin. Botticelli, the brown hamster on her head, took a strand of her hair in his mouth and tugged gently.

ᢀᢀᢀ

Andrea's home now held sixty-one hamsters, furry balls of black, brown, tan, ochre, umber, white, and orange. She went to work every day and analyzed suspicious lumps and fluids which came to her in small containers. She did autopsies on bodies that lay on steel tables. Dead people are all surface, she thought, as she cut a Y-incision in a chest, revealing what lay inside. People use surface to control what others assume about their inner selves. The dead can hide nothing.

The hamsters accompanied her in increasing numbers — to work, shopping, on other errands. She liked having them along. Their fur was a caress, the warmth and slight weight of their bodies comforting. They were always pleased to go to a new place, interested in exploring new scents and sights. People often complimented her, and Andrea liked the attention.

One day, when she wore a sweater with a floppy cowl neck and several hamsters rode on it, three lab technicians and two doctors mentioned her lovely necklace. On a day when she'd gone downtown to do errands, and hamster enthusiasm reached new heights as they clustered thickly on her shoulders, several people mentioned, often with envy, that they loved her shawl. She said, "Thank you," to each compliment. The hamsters gripped her clothing and hair and watched the world about them, their eyes dark, their noses in constant motion.

Andrea found no signs of skin cancer on her body. She wanted to check the hamsters, too, but it was difficult, now that there were over one hundred of them, to be certain she got to each one. Besides, they didn't have much exposed skin.

"You're very sensible," she said to the ones on her lap and on the couch beside her as they watched the Weather Channel. "You know about the importance of covering up when you go out into the sun." She offered sunblock to Jasmine one day, concerned about the hamsters' pink or black bare noses, but Jasmine sneezed when she sniffed the ointment and backed away.

"I'll keep it handy for you," Andrea said, "and you let me know if you want it."

ﻌﻌﻌ

Andrea hadn't been to a party for a long time. There seemed no point. She saw her friends once a week at the quilting bee. She had, she told herself, enough human contact.

One evening in late June, when the sun was fierce and the ozone hole was growing at an unprecedented rate, sparking much fascinating commentary and many panels of experts on the Weather Channel, Edna phoned Andrea to tell her about a party at the art gallery.

"It's in honour of Tim Legere, of the university art department. He's retiring. Why don't you come? I know you love his work."

Andrea did like Legere's paintings. They were landscapes, done in subtle earth tones, each detail so finely and lovingly rendered that the hills or forest or lake came alive, filled with the rustle of leaves and the scent of the wind. Hidden in each scene, subtly drawn so they seemed more a part of tree or sand or sky than separate life forms, were figures. They were part of the landscape and yet not of it, they were hidden and shy, and could only be seen if the viewer looked carefully.

Andrea glanced out her window to where the sun blazed from a clear sky. All about her, on the floor and furniture, the hamsters sat up on their hind legs and looked at her. "Okay," she said to Edna. "I'll come."

ﻌﻌﻌ

"It has been confirmed," the Weather Channel told her. "A hole in the ozone layer has opened over the North Pole. The layer has thinned in a large radius around the Pole, so that solar radiation levels are elevated as far south as Baffin Island."

It was the night of the party, and Andrea was uncertain of what to wear. She listened to the TV as she stood in front of her closet and gazed forlornly at her clothes.

"There is concern," the commentator said, "that recent droughts and unusual blights and other crop failures are due to the increased levels of solar radiation. Skin cancer rates are at a never-before-imagined high."

Another voice took over, describing new forms of eye disease and how ophthalmologists were unable to keep up with the demand for their skills. Glancing through her bedroom doorway at the TV, Andrea saw a doctor standing in front of a phacoemulsificator used for cataract surgery. The scene changed abruptly, and now she was looking at the trading floor of the Toronto Stock Exchange.

"Investors," said the commentator, "savvy enough to buy shares in companies which manufacture sunblock and other skin care products are — "

Andrea went into her living room and switched off the TV. "Our skin is being destroyed," she told the hamsters. "My skin, the earth's skin. And what's more, I have nothing to wear tonight." She sighed and sat on her sofa. Several hamsters immediately begin to climb up her legs. Their claws scratched and pinched, but the sensation was not unpleasant.

"You're smart," she said, picking up a handful of hamsters and dumping then on her lap, "to keep your skin covered. And fur is always in fashion if you're the original owner."

She gathered another armful of hamsters and, lying back, spread them over her chest. They poked their noses into her neck, and spread out to explore, eyes bright, whiskers twitching. Andrea suddenly knew what to wear.

She put on a slip, one which, although sleeveless, covered her from her shoulders to just above her knees. She stood between her sofa and a chair and the hamsters swarmed from the furniture onto her body, each finding a place to cling to. They were excited to be going out, moving their heads from side to side, their noses in constant action, up and down, up and down.

Andrea heard music and laughter as she approached the art gallery. Silhouettes of people talking and drinking could be seen inside, and light streamed out into the night through the building's large windows. She squared her shoulders, "Are we ready?" The hamsters stirred on her body, shifting their claws to get a better grip. Together, they entered the gallery.

Edna spotted Andrea as soon as she came in, and moved across the crowded floor to greet her. "It's so good to see you," she said, and leaned forward to kiss Andrea on the cheek. The others, Marlene, Jane, and Lucinda came to say hello, too. Lucinda pressed a glass of white wine into Andrea's hand.

"Here," she said. "It's sweet, just as you like it." She wrinkled her nose to show what she thought of sweet wine.

Andrea held her glass by her waist, and hamsters leaned forward to sniff it.

"You look lovely," Jane said. "I've never seen this dress." She reached to smooth her hand along Andrea's shoulder, and suddenly froze. Andrea's four friends looked at each other and back at her, their eyes wide.

"Hamsters?" Lucinda said.

There was a flurry of motion around them, as people moved from one conversation to another, refreshing their drinks at the bar along one wall, admiring Legere's paintings that hung on the other walls. A man appeared at Andrea's shoulder. She recognized him as the man in the blue-striped shirt she'd spoken to at Lucinda's party.

"Andrea," he said. "It's good to see you. You're looking lovely tonight."

Another man, the one with the ponytail, pushed his way to her side. "Hey, Andrea. Long time no see. C'mon. Let's dance." He took her hand and pulled her across the room to where a trio, two guitars and a drummer, were playing a Rolling Stones song.

The man placed one hand lightly on Andrea's shoulder. The hamsters drew back a little, and sniffed at his skin. "How," he asked, "has someone as cute as you remained hidden away for so long?" He rested his cheek against hers. "You're so soft and warm."

At the end of the dance, Andrea thanked him and moved away, even though he asked for another dance. She'd forgotten where she'd left her wine, so she got another glass and sipped it slowly, moving along the sides of the room, looking at the paintings. The hidden figures, women leaning out from behind trees, long-haired men lifting their faces above the surface of lilied lakes, women lying in grassy fields, arms stretched up to the sky, had nothing to say to her.

"His work is stunning, isn't it."

Andrea turned. A red-haired man stood beside her, gazing at a painting of a sand dune.

"Every brush stroke is a brilliant statement, all on its own," he continued. "Each colour is a separate jewel, glowing with its own unique light." He turned to face her. "But none of these works can compete with the beauty of your eyes."

Andrea smiled, and asked him if he knew where the women's room was. As she crossed the gallery to find it, she was stopped three times, once by a man who told her how lovely she looked in her dress, by a second man who said he was just leaving for a really fun party, and would she like to come along, and by a third who asked her to marry him. Each time she smiled and kept walking.

Inside the bathroom, which was mercifully empty, she took in a deep breath. The hamsters on her shoulders stood up and pressed their noses against her neck and cheeks. Their whiskers tickled and she smiled.

"It's not me," she told them. "They don't see me. But it is me who can have a good time, so I will."

She splashed water on her face and went back out to the party.

She laughed and talked, drank glass after glass of sweet wine, danced until the soles of her feet were numb. Wherever she went she was surrounded by an admiring group of men; anything she said was greeted with laughter if it was a joke, and respect if it wasn't. She saw her friends watching her, Lucinda's eyes filled with pride, Edna's with love, Jane's with surprise, but she never got a chance to speak to them. When the party was over she fended off seven offers of rides home and eleven offers to continue the party elsewhere, usually at the man's apartment, and took a cab home. She'd had a wonderful time and when she got back she collapsed face down on her bed, scattering hamsters in every direction, and cried until her eyes hurt and the skin of her face felt blistered.

ജജ

The sky quilt was almost finished. If they worked hard tonight, it would be done. The five of them sat around the frame, needles darting up and down through the three layers of material. Andrea began an arc parallel to three others she'd already quilted, the line of stitches sliding in between the leaves along one edge.

None of the hamsters had come with her tonight. They never came to the quilt evenings. Sitting beside her, Jane reached and put a hand on her shoulder. "Andrea, are you okay?"

Andrea sighed and dropped her needle. It landed on the yellow cotton sun and bounced a few times before lying still. "No. I'm not okay."

"You've been depressed since the party," Edna said.

"It's not your fault. Don't feel guilty." Andrea picked up her needle and rolled it between her thumb and forefinger. "I had a very good time."

"Why are you so low, then?" Marlene asked.

"They only liked me because of my dress." Andrea stabbed the yellow sun, again and again. "They look for cute and cuddly, and that's what they found."

She put both hands flat on the quilt. The taut material vibrated beneath her palms. "Surface is all that matters," she said. "I can do nothing about the changes to my surface, and not enough people care about the earth's surface."

"The ozone hole?" Lucinda asked.

Andrea nodded. "We can't see what we're doing. We look and we see only what we want to see. We don't see it shrivelling, drying, dying." A tear pushed against her eyelid and she wished with passion that she had a hamster or two to press against her face. "I confirmed diagnosis of three new melanomas today."

"You're scared," Lucinda said.

Andrea nodded, fighting the wetness in her eyes.

Her friends sat very still. They looked at each other, eyes meeting eyes, and then they all nodded. "There's nothing that can be done to control aging," Edna said.

"There's nothing," Jane added, "that can be done to control the stupidity of those who can't see beyond the surface."

"But," Marlene said, "we can do something about the hole in the ozone layer. People who care can do wonders."

As one the four women pulled the threads, still attached to the quilt, out of their needles, and stood. "Come with us," they said to Andrea and she followed them.

Outside it was still light, for the sun set late this time of year. Edna, beautiful tiny Edna, held her needle up above her head and passed it up and down, up and down, through the air. Lucinda, a big woman, started sewing too, and opened her mouth to sing. The others joined in, and their needles wove music into the air, a high wordless song. Andrea watched her friends, each moving her needle in and out of the sky.

She lifted hers, too, her body reaching up, and plunged it through the air. She added her voice to those of the others, and the song rose up into the atmosphere. Lucinda began to bob and sway, her red dress swinging about her ankles as she took long gliding steps across the grass. The five women danced and sang their wordless song as they sewed up the hole in the sky.

ꟷ

When Andrea got home, the house was quiet and empty. The hamsters were gone. Only Jasmine remained, sitting like a furry statue on top of the dark TV.

Andrea knew she'd miss the hamsters, but it was good to have the extra space, floors and furniture now clear and free.

She sat on her sofa and looked at the new quilt. The women had finished it, sewing long past dark, not talking but saying much. Her friends had given it to Andrea, insisting she take it, that they would start a new one the next week. She'd spread it out on her living room floor and she looked at it, the yellow sun, the blue sky, the black bird silhouettes flying fearlessly through the air.

Tiny claws moved up her leg, and she lifted it to see Jasmine on her knee. She bent her leg, spilled the black hamster onto her lap. Jasmine looked up, and began to climb, clinging to Andrea's light blue blouse.

"Are you lonely, here by yourself?" Andrea asked. "I have friends, wonderful friends. They see beyond the surface. But," and she waved her arm, almost knocking Jasmine down, "I have to wear a dress of cute hamsters to be seen by men."

Jasmine, still climbing doggedly, reached Andrea's chin. She stood up, reached with her paws and rested them on Andrea's mouth. Andrea felt a gentle pressure, the tiny pricks of claws, as Jasmine pushed on her lips, stretching them into a smile.

The smile grew, long past where Jasmine's short legs could reach. "I did get noticed, though." Her smile stretched further, until it cracked open and a great laugh surged out.

"I went to a party wearing hamsters." Andrea held Jasmine cupped in her hands, and laughed until the sun on the quilt filled her eyes.